The Cowboy's Last Rodeo

The Cowboy's Last Rodeo

A 79th Copper Mountain Rodeo Romance

Jeannie Watt

TULE
PUBLISHING

The Cowboy's Last Rodeo

Tule Publishing First Printing, August 2018

The Tule Publishing Group, LLC

First Publication by Tule Publishing Group 2018

ISBN: 978-1-949068-97-9

Chapter One

"SO MUCH FOR your season of no distractions."

Shane Marvell frowned at Tyson Bowe as they walked through the maze of trucks and horse trailers parked in the contestants' area of the Miles City, Montana, rodeo grounds on their way to the bucking chutes. Tyson gave a snort and jerked his head toward Davy Mateus's tricked-out Ford truck, where the bull rider stood talking to the woman who had caught Shane's eye more than once as he'd taped up at the trailer.

"Long black hair. Flat hat. You know…the girl you've been staring at for the past five minutes."

"She looks familiar," Shane said. Once upon a time, before he and Darcy had gotten serious, he'd made a career out of being distracted by beautiful women, but lately his only focus had been rodeo. "Any idea who she is?" He'd seen her behind the chutes during the previous rodeo in Kalispell and again in Billings, wearing that distinctive Spanish-style flat-crown hat, talking to a bull rider, but he had a feeling he knew her from somewhere else. "Some kind of reporter or something?"

"Not a clue. Sharla would smack me backward for inquiring."

That she would. Sharla ran the barrels and she also ran Tyson's life. He seemed to like it. Maybe not having to make decisions made him feel secure.

"Anyway, I'm not distracted." Although he had to admit that he could be—which meant he needed to remember what was important here.

This was his last season. His last chance to make the bucks he needed to finance his future. The future that did not include being a grunt on the family ranch forever. Oh, he'd still work there, but he'd also have an income of his own. A house of his own. Ever since he and Darcy had had the monumental discussion after he'd proposed, and she'd said no, living in his older brother's house made him feel like one of those guys who was still living in their parents' basement well into their thirties. His situation wasn't quite the same, but it was close enough to make him uncomfortable. So he was doing something about it.

"Go for it."

Shane shifted his attention to Tyson and laughed. "Go for it?"

"Yes. Do what you used to do. Be yourself, man. You're kind of scaring me lately."

"I just want to push through these last rodeos and the finals without breaking down. I can't stay on top and chase women like I used to." And heaven knew he was close to breaking down. The body that had served him so well, that had put up with eight seconds of pounding and jerking several times a week for months on end, was starting to wear. All he wanted was for it to last through the season. He was top in the standings, and if he finished on top, there was bonus money involved. Money he needed to jump-start his future.

The future he hadn't given a lot of thought to until Darcy told him she wasn't willing to share his life because he didn't really have a future.

Tyson gave him a grunt that Shane took as an indication that his friend didn't fully believe him—that he thought Shane's celibate state and low-key demeanor had more to do with Darcy than his body breaking down. Maybe it did. Her blindsiding him had served as a wake-up call. He'd dropped out of college after one year, then frittered away half of his twenties chasing buckles and big money. He'd won a decent amount of money, and spent it again on the road, chasing more buckles. Tyson, on the other hand, had gone to college. Gotten a degree in business and was settling into managing his family farm.

Depressing how far behind he was, but wallowing in should-haves would get him squat. The bonus money would help him along, but the trouble was that focusing solely on rodeo was beginning to wear, just as his body was wearing. Crazy as it was, surrounded by friends and doing something he loved, he was starting to feel isolated. Alone.

Maybe he *did* need a distraction. To act like his old self.

No…his old self had gotten him into the situation he was in—the situation he was doing his best to get out of. Currently, he was crushing his season, although he was paying a price. The stress fracture in his tibia was making it hard to walk normally, and his shoulder had seen better days. Way better days. He automatically massaged it, feeling it click in the socket as he moved his hand over the joint.

"Want me to find out who she is?" Tyson asked.

"If I want to know who she is, I'll find out myself." Shane nodded at the chute boss as he passed through the gate leading to the contestants' area.

"Chute five, Shane. Dream Machine. Tyson, chute three. Big Timber."

"Thanks." Shane moved past the chute boss to set his Barstow rigging on the wooden catwalk behind the chute, where he stood to prep the horse.

Dream Machine shifted in the chute, cocking one hind foot into a relaxed position and twitching an ear in a lazy manner as he approached. Shane ran a hand over the crest of her neck to let her know he was there and she bobbed her head. The little roan mare was a seasoned professional, and a favorite with the riders. Docile and borderline-friendly in the chute, she was known for exploding into the arena once the gate opened and bucking ferociously until the buzzer sounded eight seconds later. She always gave 100 percent, always earned a top score for her part of the ride, which meant that the end score depended on Shane and his ability to stay centered, both on the horse and in his head.

He rolled his stiff shoulder again, felt the ominous crunch of bone on bone, then set the Barstow rigging on the horse's withers. Tyson was already on the other side of the gate, ready to pull the latigo once Shane used the wire hook to draw the cinch under the horse to his side. They worked silently, as did the cowboys in the chutes on either side. Everyone was getting into their heads in their own way. And yet, as Shane pulled the laces on his glove, he wondered once again about the dark-haired woman with the thing for bull riders.

And then he remembered where he'd seen her. College rodeo finals. Bozeman. Many years ago. Mitch Etch, the champion saddle bronc rider, was her brother. She'd helped him pull the rigging on the bronc during the competition, and it'd been damned hard not to admire the masterful way she'd done it.

Now he kind of wished he'd gotten her name.

~

"MS. EET...ZUH...BERRY?" THE bull rider glanced up from Ella's business card to give her a hopeful look and she had to stifle a smile. Eat the berry? That was a new twist on her name. When her great-grandfather had insisted on keeping the traditional spelling of his Basque surname after emigrating from the old country, he'd sentenced his family to a life of correcting both spelling and pronunciation. Etxeberri didn't exactly trip off the tongue unless you happened to live in the parts of Nevada and Idaho where the Basque had settled.

"Etch-eh-berry. The 'x' is pronounced as 'chuh.'"

The bull rider once again studied the card. "Right."

"Just call me Ella Etch. It's easier." She'd been an Etch all her life, as had her younger brothers, father and stepmom. Her stepsister had kept her late father's surname, and many was the time that Ella had envied Finley her simple last name. Everyone could pronounce—and spell—James.

The big cowboy in front of her, her second interview of the day, gave her a crooked smile and she noticed he had a chipped front tooth. Her eldest brother, Joe, had no front teeth—although he now had a fine set of implants.

"How about I just call you Ella? I only know one. That's you." He gave her a look that was apparently supposed to let her know that was special.

"Ella it is."

The music from the grand entry faded and the national anthem began to play. The bull rider pulled off his hat and Ella put her hand over her heart as they turned together to face the arena. Restless broncs shifted in their chutes while the anthem played, adding muffled metallic clangs to the singer's beautiful a cappella rendition of the song.

After the anthem ended and the crowd erupted into

cheers, the bull rider put his hat back in place and turned his attention to Ella. "Now what is it you want to talk about exactly?"

"The risks you take as part of your chosen profession."

He gave her a slow smile, his eyes lighting up. She'd seen that same look on her brothers' faces too many times to count. And Finley…she wasn't going there. Some people were simply addicted to risk. Ella wanted to know why.

"What about it?"

She smiled at him. "Anything you want to tell me. But maybe we could start with your name."

"T.J. Bodin." He settled his hands on his trophy buckle, rocking on his heels. "You going to take notes?"

He looked as if he really wanted her to take notes, unlike a lot of cowboys, who preferred to give almost all monosyllabic replies to her questions.

Ella pushed a few dark strands off her face and tucked them behind her ear. "A few, just to keep you guys straight. At this point of my research, I'm gathering preliminary information to help me focus my research. Later, if people are willing, I'll ask for a more in-depth interview, probably by phone or Skype." *If* she got her research grant and proceeded on with her studies. If she didn't get the grant…she had no idea what she was going to do. Find a job in a competitive field, probably. Or end up wearing a paper hat. Whatever it took to get by until she did get funding and earned her next degree.

"And this is for…"

"My master's thesis." In sports psychology, but she didn't generally mention that immediately, as it tended to make people more self-conscious about the answers they gave. And a self-conscious cowboy was usually a silent cowboy. Even her brothers clammed up when they thought she was 'probing their psyches' as Joe liked to call it. Like she wanted to know what went on in their heads.

All right, she *did* want to know—or rather, she wanted to know why she didn't have the same fearless nature as the rest of the family. Why she was the one who kept counting the cost and hesitating to the point that she was beginning to feel as if she was watching life instead of living it.

She couldn't pinpoint when she'd started to feel restless, when she began to wonder if she'd allowed the pendulum to swing too far toward the safe side of life—oddly, she suspected it had been while her brother had been recovering from the injury that should have killed him—but she could, however, pinpoint the exact moment she realized she was going to do something about her overly cautious nature. During the interview for the research assistantship she *hadn't* gotten, the one she'd hoped would help finance graduate school, so she didn't have to take out more loans, the professor had asked about her brothers, both alums of the university. When she'd finished updating him, he'd said, "You have a fascinating family." She'd smiled and nodded and felt hopeful at his making such a personal observation...until his expression had shifted and he added, "You're different from your brothers."

It hadn't been a compliment.

And the woman he'd hired as research assistant for his study into the psychology of extreme athletics? She turned out to be a base jumper who didn't have anything close to the academic credentials Ella had. But she had street cred, which Ella did not.

That had stung, but it had also lit a fire under her, and for the first time since entering her kindergarten classroom, Ella wasn't heading off to school at the end of August. Nope. She was going to continue following the rodeo circuit as she tried to find out more about herself as well as the guys she was interviewing. Did these guys feel the same hesitation before taking big risks that she did, but somehow manage to overcome it? If so, how?

It wasn't like she was a chicken when push came to shove. She could rope and ride better than most. She'd once faced down a cougar who'd been stalking the lambs before chasing it off with a shovel. She had chops—she just needed to use them.

She turned her attention back to the bull rider. "I know you need to prepare, but if you could spare a few minutes for a handful of questions, I'd appreciate it."

The muscles under the guy's T-shirt rippled as he shrugged. He was big for a bull rider. "Sure. I have time."

She pulled her small notebook out of her back pocket

and retrieved the pencil from behind her ear. Her dad always kept his pencils there while he worked, and so did she. "Let's start with your age and hometown."

T.J. became serious. "I'm twenty-two and was born in Wisdom. My folks run a tire store there."

"So you're not from a ranching background."

His expression became vaguely defensive. "Like more than half these guys on the circuit."

"Trust me. I understand that there aren't that many people who can make a living ranching. Someone has to have a real job to make ends meet."

"Yeah, I—" He lifted his chin as the gate of the bucking chute swung open, then let out a low whistle. "Nice horse."

Nice cowboy.

The little roan mare was doing her job and then some, but the guy on top, leaning back so far that his head was touching the mare's tail, spurring in a perfect rhythm, was doing just as well in Ella's opinion. The buzzer sounded, and the little horse continued to buck. The cowboy took a double grip and worked his glove free while the pickup man came into position, then slick as can be the cowboy swung off the horse, released his grip on the pickup man and landed on his feet. The crowd went nuts.

"You know him?" Ella asked.

"Shane Marvell?" T.J. laughed. "Last year he rode with a cast on his free arm due to a broken wrist. Nearly knocked himself out with it a time or two." The bull rider gave her a crooked smile that had probably melted the heart of more than one buckle bunny. "But back to me..."

And back to T.J. it was, as he continued to expound on his favorite subject—himself. Ella nodded and jotted down notes, thinking she wouldn't have to contact him for a deeper interview because he was giving her all he had with this one. But he was a nice guy and had an interesting take on life. And danger.

She was just closing her notebook when T.J. lifted his chin, just as he had when they'd stopped to watch the bronc rides. But this time he was looking at something behind her, so Ella automatically glanced over her shoulder and found herself looking into an intense pair of blue eyes. Blue that bordered on sapphire. Or maybe the tan on the guy's face simply made his eyes look bluer than normal.

"Shane," T.J. said from behind her. "I was just telling Ella about you."

Ella felt a flush rising in her cheeks for no reason she could think of. The man had just had a hellacious ride, scoring in the upper eighties, but it wasn't that. Something about him made her feel like smoothing her hair to make sure that the annoying wisps that curled around her face hadn't escaped her braid. Instead she gripped her pencil a little tighter.

"What exactly were you telling Ella?" Shane asked.

"About how you almost knocked yourself out with your cast last year."

Shane smiled, his cheeks creasing pleasantly, which made him look crazy sexy, and Ella had a feeling he knew it. "More than once." He kept his eyes on her as he spoke, as if there was some mystery about her that he wanted to solve, which only made her face feel warmer. What the hell?

"Do a lot of guys ride with casts?" she asked, already knowing the answer. Her brother had done just that at the end of his last season before sanity overtook him and he retired to go back to college, and when she'd told him he was stupid for risking the use of his wrist, he'd named at least five guys who'd done the same and had ended up with a working joint. Or a mostly working joint.

"I know a few." His gaze traveled over her face. "By the way, I'm Shane Marvell."

"Ella Etxeberri."

"You should see how it's spelled," T.J. said helpfully.

The corner of Shane's mouth twitched as he held out a hand. "Nice to meet you, Ella. I remember you from college finals years ago. You helped your bother with his rigging."

She was stunned that he would remember such a thing. "Mitch was particular." And a touch superstitious. If Ella pulled the rigging he knew it was right, but she'd also been something of a good luck charm to him. Too bad she hadn't been there during the rodeo where he'd almost died. She'd been working on a paper that was getting the best of her when she got the news of the accident.

"I remember your hat. It's distinctive."

Her hat? Well, so much for being flattered.

She reached up to touch the black felt hat with the cream-colored ribbon on the edge of the brim and around the base of the crown. The Spanish-style hats favored by vaqueros were common in Nevada, but not so common in Montana, where cowboys favored classic cattlemen styles.

"We Nevadans love our flat hats."

"I'm curious as to what a Nevadan is doing on the east side of Montana?"

He was curious. She could see it in the way he was studying her, which made her want to shift self-consciously.

"Research," T.J. said easily. "Ella is working on her master's and interviewing bull riders about risk."

"You don't say." Shane shifted the rigging he carried to his other hand. His jeans were still dusty from the arena, as were the batwing chaps he was carrying over one shoulder. "Bull riders."

T.J. once again hooked his thumbs behind his trophy buckle, which happened to read *Champion Bull Rider Miles City 2017*. "Yeah. Because she wants to interview people who actually take risks."

Shane Marvell's expression went hard, and Ella, who wasn't certain if he was serious or not, quickly interjected, "I'm interviewing bull riders because they take the most obvious risks, both on top of the animal and after they hit the dirt." She refrained from saying anything about bronc riders also taking great risks, because it sounded condescending. The truth was, she shied away from bareback riders because of what had happened to Mitch.

"Fair enough." Shane touched the brim of his dusty hat. "Nice to meet you, Ella."

She watched him walk away, toward the parking area, feeling the strangest sense of disappointment. Why?

"I've got to get to my stretching," T.J. said. "Good talking to you, and if you need more information, give a shout."

"Will do."

"And friend me on Facebook," he called after her.

Oh, yeah. For sure.

As she headed back to her truck, parked next to the trailer belonging to the barrel-racing sisters she was traveling with, she once again caught sight of Shane Marvell talking to another guy carrying a bareback rigging.

Damn but he was sexy. And he remembered her from a rodeo at least seven years ago. Surely it was more than the hat. She reached up to touch the beribboned felt brim and pull it down a little more snugly over her eyes.

She really, really wanted it to be more than the hat.

"ARE YOU COMING?" Avery Glenn held a sparkly earring shaped like a cowboy boot up to one side of her face and a miniature silver lariat earring to the other.

"The boot," Ella said automatically, stepping back to give Avery a little more room to pull on her jeans. The teardrop camper was small, small, small, but whenever she and the Glenn sisters attended the same rodeos, they invited her to roll out her sleeping bag on the floor between the cushioned benches they slept on.

"And I should probably write up my notes."

Avery's younger sister, Jenna, stuck her head out of the postage-stamp size bathroom. "You're coming. I want to hear about your bull rider interviews."

"You aren't going to hear anything about my bull rider interviews," Ella said with mock sternness. "Confidentiality and all that."

Jenna blew a raspberry and shut the door again. She was twenty-one and one of the best barrel racers on the circuit. She was also awkward and shy around anyone who wasn't a friend or family, but that didn't keep her from dreaming about having a bull rider sweep her off her feet someday. Ella didn't have the heart to tell her that maybe she'd be better off finding someone a bit more stable in terms of both profession and personal health. Mainly because she understood the attraction. Why else would she keep replaying the scene with Shane Marvell in her head and tamping down the feeling that maybe she should have said something before he walked away?

What?

And better yet, why?

She tried to remember another time she'd had such a crazy physical response to a guy she'd met for the first time and couldn't, but the keyword there was *physical.* There was something about him, apparently, that struck a chord with her hormones. Maybe some deep genetic memory that was telling her more primal self that this was a good guy to make children with. That he had strong genes that would mesh well with her own.

"What?" Avery asked in an amused voice as she sat on the sofa/bed before pulling on a pink boot.

Ella realized then that she was smiling. She gave her head a dismissive shake. "Just thinking about genetics."

"And smiling." Avery reached for her other boot. "You get way too much joy from research."

"Bull rider research," Jenna called from the john. "Of course, she gets joy from it." She opened the bathroom door and Ella moved to the right so that she had room to close the door again.

"You look good," Ella said. She wore a white cold-shoulder T-shirt, dark jeans and had pulled her long blonde hair into a low ponytail. She wasn't a bling gal like her sister, but the simple outfit suited her.

"Put on some earrings," Avery suggested.

"I feel like I have three eyes as it is," Jenna said before lifting her chin, "but I'm going to have a social life if it kills me."

"Bluff," Ella said. "Pretend you're confident and people will believe it."

"Until I start stuttering and blushing and all that crap."

"Smile mysteriously," Avery suggested. "Most guys want to do all the talking anyway."

An image of T.J. shot into Ella's head. After starting out cautiously, he'd warmed up to his subject—himself. But he wasn't a bad guy. Just young. And full of himself.

"What's it to be?" Avery asked as she got to her feet. "Notes or social life?"

Ella hesitated for a little less than a nanosecond. "Social life." She wanted to set a good example for Jenna. And, truth be told, she wanted to lay eyes on Shane Marvell again. Not because she wanted to ogle him, but because she wanted to evaluate her reaction to him. Her response had given her pause. Had she been justified in her response, or had it simply been the heat of the afternoon that left her all hot and bothered?

SHANE WAS GETTING tired of being a third wheel with Tyson and Sharla, especially since Sharla didn't particularly care for him, or for anyone who was close to Tyson, so instead of tagging along with his best friend and taking snide hits all night, he headed to the local roadhouse with two other bronc riders. He rarely drank before a ride. He liked alcohol well enough, but hangovers screwed with his timing and he wasn't about to let his love of single malt interfere with his future ability to *buy* single malt during the off-season.

They were just getting out of the truck after parking in the gravel lot behind the bar when someone hailed them. T.J. For all of his trash talk, the kid was okay. He just got a kick out of pushing buttons and swaggering. Like he'd tried to push a button after introducing Shane to Ella Etch, who was even more intriguing up close than she'd been at a distance. Intriguing and beautiful. She had a quiet dignity—the kind that came from knowing you're good at something—but she hadn't been at ease when they'd talked. It was almost as if being close to him put her off her game.

Well, now he knew why he kept seeing her at rodeos. There was a core group of competitors who traveled the Montana circuit, but there were also a lot of local guys who didn't have the time, money or inclination to travel to a new rodeo every week, so they only competed in a few close to home. That would give her new subjects for research. It made sense.

But bull riders? Yeah. They were a special breed, but it didn't take any more guts to get on a bull than a bareback bronc. There was a reason that there were fewer competitors in bareback than in any other event. It was brutal in a way the other events weren't and if a guy didn't have proper conditioning, and a proper mindset, he may as well kiss his chances goodbye.

Today's ride had been phenomenal, and he couldn't help but wonder if it was because he'd been distracted by Ella Etxeberri—to the point that he hadn't overthought his performance, because he'd been thinking about her. He'd relaxed and the resulting score had put him firmly in the top spot. And then fate had put her directly in his path.

He ordered a Coke and stepped to the side of the room and surveyed the crowd while his bronc rider friends started circulating. He'd join them soon enough, but right now he wanted to see if a certain researcher had decided to join the rodeo after-party, or if she'd already hit the road.

It didn't take long for him to spot her, on the opposite side of the room, sitting with Avery Glenn. Shane leaned his shoulder against the wall, holding his Coke close to his chest to keep from wearing it as people pushed past him. Damn but she was something, with that long black hair tumbling down her back, still wavy from the loose braid she'd had it in earlier. Avery was all spangles, like usual, and her younger sister, whom he didn't know, was the exact opposite. Ella was somewhere in between, but she still caught his eye more than Avery. Was she looking for a party? Or a research subject?

He smiled to himself. He could be a subject. He wasn't a bull rider, but he had a feeling that the vibe he'd felt while talking to Ella hadn't been one-sided. Maybe Tyson was right. Maybe he needed to start acting like his old self, allow himself a distraction or two.

Maybe he needed to talk Ella Etxeberri into doing research on a bronc rider.

Chapter Two

ELLA HAD SPOTTED Shane Marvell standing near the bar the minute she walked in the door. He'd been alonethen, but T.J. and another guy had joined him by the time their drinks arrived. Fortuitously, Jenna had chosen a table where she could maintain her view of the guy and try to figure out what the deal was with him. Why he jangled her nerves the way he did.

If someone had asked her a couple days ago if she had a type, she would have said, "Sure. Dark-haired, high cheekbones, tall, muscular." Like every guy she'd ever dated.

Shane Marvell had the cheekbones, but that was where the resemblance ended. He was of average height, his hair closer to blond than brown. And his body...well, it was something all right, all hard and muscular, but it was the lean, wiry muscle that rough-stock riders developed, not the bulk of a gym rat. Not that she was looking for a gym rat, but she'd always dated guys who looked like they worked out regularly. Steer wrestler types. Shane Marvell had a different look, but there was no denying it stirred something within her.

"Who's that guy you're watching?" Jenna asked just as Shane turned and scanned the crowd as if looking for someone. Ella quickly dropped her gaze.

"That's Shane Marvell," her sister answered for Ella. "We competed in high school rodeo."

"I noticed him at some of the earlier rodeos," Jenna said. She'd finished her dental assistant training in late June and had joined Avery on the circuit about the same time Ella had, in mid-July.

Ella took a sip of beer, trying to not sound like she wanted to pump her friend for information. She had some pride, after all. "I met him today when I was doing an interview."

"Is he your next victim?" Jenna asked.

He could be, her trouble-making inner voice whispered to her. *You are doing preliminary work to narrow down the scope of your study...why not see what a bronc rider has to say?*

"I'm not sure. I narrowed my subjects to bull riders."

"Expand your horizons," Avery said dryly.

Tempting. A good excuse to...talk.

And technically she hadn't only spoken to bull riders. She'd also interviewed bullfighters and a few weeks ago she'd talked to a very determined woman working toward her pro ticket in saddle bronc riding. When she'd asked CJ Cooper about her choices in life, the woman had said she didn't want to look back on her life with regret because she let what other people might think dictate her choices.

Excellent advice, Ms. Cooper.

Ella blew out a breath as she once again focused on the guy leaning against the wall on the other side of the room. Why wasn't every woman in the room staring at him, since he was the hottest guy there? No. Wait. There *were* a lot of women studying him. And rightly so.

"Do you know anything about him?" she asked Avery after finally tearing her gaze away. So much for pride.

Her friend shrugged. "I know he comes from the Marietta area, and he's hot as hell. But I haven't seen him since high school, so no, I don't know much else."

Not surprising, since Avery had attended the University of Nevada, Reno, where she and Ella had met, and had only been back in Montana for a matter of months.

Avery took a sip of her margarita. "Well?"

Ella didn't ask, *"Well what?"* She knew what. She and Avery had discussed the changes she was making in her life. What a perfect opportunity to put up or shut up. "I guess I can just go over there and ask him for an interview."

"You could do that," Avery agreed. Jenna's gaze bounced between the two of them as Avery waited for Ella to either man up or chicken out. "Or buy him a drink, if you wanted to go really wild. You know—be direct."

The interview felt safer. Baby steps and all that. Ella had never been all that comfortable initiating matters, but this summer was all about change. And exploration.

Ella pushed back her chair as she stood. She could do

this. He was no more frightening than a lamb-stalking cougar.

Not much anyway.

"Good luck," Jenna murmured as Ella picked up her drink. With her heart beating faster than she'd like, she started making her way across the room. This was part of her new life adventure. Taking chances she wouldn't normally take. And if she got shot down, it wouldn't be the end of the world, because, hey, she never had to see Shane Marvell again.

"LOOK WHO'S COMING to see me," T.J. said from behind Shane. Shane, who hadn't realized the bull rider had just emerged from the billiard room, hoped that wasn't true. T.J.'d had his shot. But judging from the way Ella was zeroing in on him as she approached, Shane had a hunch that T.J. was wrong.

"I think she's coming to interview me," Shane said loud enough for her to hear.

"I am," she agreed giving T.J. a sympathetic smile.

"A bronc rider?" T.J. said in mock outrage.

Ella gave a what-can-I-say shrug. "It's true," she said placatingly.

"Well, if you want another real interview, you know where to find me."

"I'll keep that in mind," she said before turning her attention back to Shane as T.J. headed into the billiard room again. "Do you think we could find a quiet corner?"

Shane shook his head. "No. But we could step outside."

"Good idea." Her voice held a husky note, which made him believe that the vibe he'd felt earlier that day was not one-sided. Ella was as tuned in to him as he was to her. It was a heady feeling after months of celibacy. Maybe he was finally ready to move on.

The night was warm, but the air felt remarkably cool as Shane held open the side entrance so that Ella could precede him out the door. As they left the noise and the press of the crowd, Shane pulled a deep breath of fresh air into his lungs. Maybe he was getting old, but crowded bars were starting to make him feel claustrophobic. Ella also seemed to appreciate the openness of the parking lot. She dropped her head back to look at the stars, which were washed out by the lights of town. Nothing like the stars at home on the Marvell Cattle Company ranch.

"Nice night," she murmured.

Shane perched a hip against the bumper of a nearby truck and folded his arms over his chest before asking the zillion-dollar question. "You seemed pretty adamant about sticking with bull riders earlier."

"I want to keep my research focused." Ella paused to moisten her lips before adding, "But I see no harm in getting additional data to inform my study."

"Additional data." Shane cocked his head at her. "Was

that the only reason you crossed the room?" Ella held his gaze without faltering, but he saw her throat move and if he wasn't mistaken, her cheeks were slightly pinker than before. Interesting for a woman who interviewed rodeo riders and helped rig bucking broncs. "Tell me it wasn't for T.J.," he deadpanned.

She bit her lip, then lost the battle and gave a smile that lit her eyes and transformed her face from beautiful to breathtaking in the process. "Not to be rude, but no. It wasn't for T.J."

It took Shane a second to find his voice. He felt almost gut-punched by his reaction to her. "Good. Then we can talk."

"You got a thing against T.J.?"

"Not one. But I can't see us being interested in the same women."

"Interested?" she asked, her voice taking on a cool edge, even though he didn't think she was feeling all that cool. "We've met once for maybe two minutes."

"Yet you crossed a crowded bar to seek me out."

Her chin lifted as her smile faded. "To ask you about an interview."

He didn't reply, and after an awkward beat of silence, Ella dropped her gaze to the toe of her rough-out boot. A utilitarian boot, unlike the fancy boots most of the women inside the bar were wearing. Utilitarian, but somehow sexy on her. She looked up at him again, the expression in her warm hazel eyes utterly serious.

"That's a lie."

"Is it now?" He was surprised at the admission. He'd thought he'd have to work harder.

"A lie and an easy way out."

He took a chance and reached out to lightly touch her upper arm. She didn't move away, so he allowed his fingers to slide down to her elbow, where they stayed, keeping a point of contact between them. "Easy way out of what?"

She hesitated, then lifted her chin in a get-down-to-business expression that made him believe she'd decided to say exactly what was on her mind. "Getting answers to a burning question."

"Which is?"

Ella canted her head to one side and studied him in a way that made him feel borderline self-conscious—and he rarely felt self-conscious. Her eyebrows lifted a fraction of an inch, then she said in a musing, almost clinical tone, "What it is about you that draws my eye."

Her candid answer made him smile. Was this what it was like to flirt with a scientist? If so, he kind of liked it.

He stroked his thumb over the firm muscle of her arm and she eased half a step closer. Close enough that a light floral scent teased his nostrils. Now he took half a step closer and slid his free hand up her other arm, bringing their faces that much closer, but Ella didn't so much as lean back. If anything she leaned toward him.

His heart was beating a steady rhythm of anticipation as she continued to study him. "I'm not going to kiss you," she murmured.

Now he smiled for real. "What makes you think you'll get a chance?"

Ella shrugged, her arm moving beneath his palm. "Analysis of the data. Dilated pupils, change of breathing pattern. If I put my hand on your chest, your heart would be beating harder."

"Or so you hypothesize." *Thank you, Mrs. Anderson, for hammering the scientific method into me in seventh grade.*

She put her palm on his chest, dead center, and spread her fingers as she closed her eyes. Shane wondered if she felt the skip in his heartbeat when she made contact. "My hypothesis is correct."

Her lips parted ever so slightly and that was all the invitation Shane needed. He brought his mouth down close to hers, his grip tightening at her elbows, although he made no move to pull her closer. "I think you should kiss me," he whispered against her lips. He felt her lean toward him.

"If I kiss you, I can't interview you."

"Conflict of interest?"

"Got it in one." She leaned back, her dark gaze searching his face. "And I think I do want to interview you."

"Even though I'm not a bull rider?"

"I'm looking at broadening my scope."

"And after the interview?"

"Depends on whether I'll need to talk to you again. Right now I'm collecting preliminary data to write a grant proposal to subsidize my study."

"Preliminary data." He smiled down at her. "Hot."

She laughed and it made him want to kiss her even more than he had a few seconds ago when her lips had been a whisper away from his. "Maybe we can talk tomorrow. After the short go. I don't want to mess with your head before it."

"Yeah. I think that would work. I'm traveling alone." Because Sharla wasn't going to let Tyson, his former travel buddy, out of her sight. "Where are you heading after this rodeo?"

"I'm going to South Dakota with my friends."

"I'm going to Plains."

Ella gave a nod. "Then we'd better hook up tomorrow."

He wanted to hook up now. To pull her up against the length of him and explore that beautiful mouth, inside and out. And if he did that, he may scare her off forever. He exhaled sharply and stepped back, letting his hands drop back to his sides. "I'll see you after the short go. At the Glenn trailer?"

"You know the trailer?"

"It's the same one Avery's family crammed into during the high school rodeo season. Yeah. I know it. It's like a clown car."

Ella laughed, then folded her arms over her chest as she took a casual step back. Her expression grew serious as she said, "Great. I'll…uh…see you then."

Now that there was some distance between them, she seemed less at ease, as if she was wondering what the hell had just happened between them.

Shane smiled, resisted the urge to move closer again, and instead reached past her to open the door to the bar, thus giving her the easy escape she so obviously wanted. "Yeah. See you then."

DEAR HEAVENS. SHE'D almost kissed a total stranger. It'd been all she could do *not* to kiss a total stranger. She blew out a shaky breath as she edged between two big cowboys. Maybe she *should* have kissed a stranger. Already pangs of regret were battling with the sense of having made a narrow escape.

She'd see him tomorrow. It wasn't like he was walking out of her life before she could find out what it was like to kiss him—if she decided she wanted to, of course.

She felt both alive and a little light-headed as she wound her way through the crowded bar toward the table where Avery and Jenna still sat. The two formerly empty chairs were now filled with a couple of hunky cowboys. Jenna was smiling nervously and nodding a little too vigorously, but hey, she was out there, doing what she said she was going to do. She and Jenna were both taking some chances tonight. And that was good.

Of course it was.

Although…she was still working through the kissing-the-stranger thing. This was supposed to be her summer of freedom and exploration, but now that she was actually indulging herself, she was also debating her ability to handle situations she'd never been in before.

No. She wasn't. She wouldn't let self-doubt ruin things.

"Hey," Avery said with a bright smile. "Let's find you a chair."

"I think you may as well say, 'Let's find you a gold nugget.' There aren't any."

"I'll get one." The bigger of the two cowboys got to his feet and a few seconds later, returned with a chair.

"Thank you," Ella said, gratefully taking a seat. Her knees quite literally felt weak.

"Where've you been?" Avery asked in a low aside once Ella had squeezed in next to her.

"Expanding my horizons."

Avery gave a small snort. "No kidding. How'd that go?"

Ella was searching for an answer she could live with when her phone buzzed in her pocket and she shifted sideways in her seat to dig it out. Finley. Her heart rate bumped. Her sister never called to shoot the breeze or gossip. That was what texting was for. Nope. Finley only called in the event of an emergency.

Ella took the call, told her sister to hang on while she got to somewhere quiet, then slipped out of her chair. A few seconds later, thanks to the table's proximity to the door, she was once again outside in the parking lot. Only this time she didn't feel the anticipation of possible erotic adventure lying ahead. This time she felt nothing but dread.

"What's going on?"

"The good news is that he's going to recover."

Ella's heart almost stopped. "Who's going to recover?"

"Mitch."

She really, really wished this was the first time she'd gotten a call like this, but the truth was that with Joseba, Mitch and Finley, not to mention her father, Frank, she'd received more than her share.

"Is he in the hospital?"

"Yes, but it's no longer life-threatening."

"Give me the story." Ella ran a hand under her hair and massaged the back of her neck.

"Smoke inhalation and a shoulder injury. It was a structure fire and he made a rescue."

"Kittens?" Ella asked weakly. Once he'd risked his life for kittens.

"No. One of the new firefighters—I can't remember his name—went in when he shouldn't have and Mitch went in after him. The roof collapsed. He got hit by some debris, but the biggest danger was the smoke inhalation. He's breathing on his own now."

Ella let out a sigh and bunched the hair at the back of her neck into her fist. Of her siblings, she was closest to Mitch.

When the bronc had kicked him in the head and no one knew whether or not he'd pull through, Ella hadn't known how she could possibly go on. And then, when he'd made a miraculous recovery, he'd become chief of the local volunteer fire department. Because, you know, an Etch wouldn't want to have a side job that *didn't* involve the potential for danger.

"I can be there by tomorrow evening if I leave tonight."

"You don't have to come home…but Mom would appreciate it."

"I know." Her parents were fine with their kids going their own way, doing their own thing, but when trouble struck, the family came together and formed a tight unit. And how could she not go home and prop up Mitch? Again. "I think I can make Billings if I leave right now, then start from there in the morning."

"Don't drive if you're tired."

Ella gave a short laugh. She felt wide awake. Something about that near miss with Shane Marvell. "I'll be fine." Or as fine as she could be while worried about her brother. "I'll text when I get there."

Ella ended the call and dropped her head back to once again stare up at the stars. This was her life. Her family couldn't help the way they were, so she could either be one of them or be an outsider. She was trying damned hard to be one of them.

Which meant that she should have kissed the cowboy when she'd had the chance.

Chapter Three

SHANE PROPPED HIS boot on the running board of his truck and started wrapping laces around the leather at the ankle, where it was worn and floppy from tying on his boots several times a week. The alternative was for his boots to come off during the ride, and that did no one any good.

He finished the first boot and started the second. After the short go was over, he'd pack up and drive home to Paradise Valley, where his home ranch, the Marvell Cattle Company, was located. He would not be answering questions from Ella about the risks he chose to take, because Ella had a family emergency and had taken off the night before.

He was disappointed, even as he tried to convince himself that he had no reason to feel that way. The thing was, she was the first woman he'd looked twice at since Darcy dumped him, and he couldn't help but think that was a good thing.

He wished like hell that he knew her well enough to ask Avery for her number, so he could text her, see if all was well, but he didn't, and he wasn't going to push matters. He gave his bootlaces a good tug, then knotted them tightly. He'd once had a boot come off due to a loose knot. That was never happening again.

He shrugged into his vest, swung his chaps over his shoulder, grabbed his rigging and headed for the chutes. It'd been months since he'd thought of anything except his next ride, or his lost future with Darcy, but a few minutes with Ella Etxeberri had jerked him out of his rut. He owed her for that.

He just didn't know if he'd ever have the chance to repay her.

Boone Telford, a guy he'd gone to school with in Marietta, gave him a nod as he approached the chutes. "Hey, Shane. Great ride yesterday. You gave me something to shoot for."

And the guy had come damned close to his target, with a score only one point below Shane's. "Hoping to hold you at bay today, Boone." And he'd have to keep doing that if he hoped to win the end-of-season bonus.

Boone gave him one of his open smiles. "Good luck with that." The crazy thing was that Boone meant it. He was that rarest of breeds—a truly good guy.

Tyson hadn't made his ride the day before, so he and Sharla had pulled out that morning. They'd hook up again in Plains, Montana, at the end of the week—if Sharla let Tyson out, that was.

Why the hell couldn't Tyson see that Sharla was all

about control and jealousy? That she wasn't exactly a nice person?

Maybe for the same reason you didn't realize what was going on with Darcy?

He hadn't made any kind of mistake about Darcy's character, but he had honestly thought they were on the same page. It'd killed him to discover they were not. It had been even worse when he had to admit that she had a point. He had nothing to offer. Just a minimum-wage job on the family ranch…well, maybe a little below minimum wage. He wasn't even in a position to buy a trailer to put on his own chunk of ground there.

But now he was, and if he won the bonus money at the end of the season, he'd be able to buy a double-wide.

But minimum wage and a double-wide still didn't seem like much of a deal to him. Nope. He was going to have to go back to school. Learn a trade, then do what he could to make up for all the years he'd spent enjoying himself instead of planning for a future.

SHANE MARVELL WON his event in Miles City. Ella had checked the standings after stopping for gas in Elko. Judging from the scores, Boone Telford had given him a run for his money, and if Ella interviewed Shane, she'd interview Boone, too, since he also seemed to be on fire.

If she interviewed Shane. Now that she was back in Nevada, in her home stomping grounds, Montana seemed a long way away. And it still seemed like she should be heading off to school, as she'd done every year for the past nineteen years.

After leaving the freeway at Winnemucca, she drove straight to the hospital—an all too familiar trip having grown up with her rowdy brothers—and was met by her sister who pulled her into a hug as she walked into the lobby. Ella hugged her back. Hard. They were polar opposites, she and her half-sister—Finley was fair and Ella was dark; Finley was a spitfire and Ella was introspective. But when push came to shove, they were equal in the backbone department. Neither of them backed away from trouble that couldn't be avoided—although Finley had been known to stand tall against trouble that could be avoided.

"You didn't have to come, but I'm glad you did."

"Where's Mom?"

"She's in Walmart with her long shopping list." The family ranch was seventy miles from town, so every trip to town was used to stock up. "They're going to release Mitch in a few hours."

"Can I see him now?"

"I'll show you the way." Finley stepped back and gave Ella a once-over. "You're looking good, by the way. Playing hooky suits you."

Before Ella could answer, Finley started down the hall, her boot heels clicking on the tile. Halfway down the corridor, she stopped in front of a partially open door. "I'll let you guys have some alone time, because once Mom gets here, there'll be no such thing."

"Dad's on the ranch?"

"He and Joe left about an hour ago."

"Thanks, Fin." Ella eased the door open a little more and peeked around the curtain. Her brother lay propped against pillows.

"Hey," he said as she came into the room. His face was pale beneath his tan, and he had an abrasion across his cheek, but he managed his usual cocky smile. "Ella."

"Mitch." She stood for a moment, staring at him, flashing back to the last time she'd visited him in this hospital, when he'd almost died. He really needed to stop doing this. But he wouldn't.

"You didn't have to come, you know." Mitch gestured at his bound-up shoulder with his free hand, barely disguising his wince of pain. "It's not life-threatening."

Ella smiled without answering. She *did* have to come. After almost losing him two years ago, not coming wasn't an option. Besides, what kind of sister didn't come home after her brother was injured? Maybe she'd feel less of a need to check on those that she loved and make certain they were all right sometime in the future, but for right now, she was doing exactly what she needed to do.

"I came for me." An answer she knew he could accept.

He smiled back at her and relaxed against the pillows. "About time you started doing something for you, although this isn't what I would have chosen."

"You probably would have chosen to go hang gliding or BASE jumping?" Both of which he had done in college when he wasn't busy with his rodeo season. It was surprising that he managed to get his agriculture degree, but he had and was putting it to use on the ranch. When he wasn't in the hospital.

"No. I'm slowing down."

"Right." She hadn't seen any pigs fly by, so she didn't believe him.

"No. Really. I'm easing into a new phase of my life."

That sounded eerily similar to what she was doing, only she had a feeling she was moving in the opposite direction from her brother. He was talking about slowing down and she was thinking about speeding up.

"Is there a reason? I mean...did you have some kind of awakening? Or did the decision just creep up on you?" Ella asked as she came closer.

"Pretty much crept up and ambushed me. I realized that I wasn't getting any younger, and the folks needed me. Ironically, I was thinking of how I was becoming less impulsive when I did this." He smiled, apparently unfazed by his near miss. "I guess I'm a work in progress."

"Aren't we all?" She perched on the edge of the chair next to the bed, trying to relax, even though she hated hospitals. It was so easy to flash back to the tense family vigils held after his rodeo wreck.

"I know what you're thinking," Mitch said mildly. "And you need to stop."

"It's hard."

"Well, for your information, everyone is a little wigged out by *you* not going back to school this fall."

Nice change of subject. Ella went with it. "I'll go back when it's time."

"When will that be?"

Ella let out a breath and fiddled with the small rip in her jeans. "I don't know. I'm just taking time off."

"I gotta tell you, I'm impressed that you're taking a semester off."

"I…think I might have imploded if I hadn't. I couldn't believe I didn't get that research assistantship. I mean…" she gave a frustrated gesture "…I was the best candidate. Hands down. But he chose someone who lived the life rather than someone who had studied it."

"He made a mistake."

"Yeah. He did." But his mistake had convinced her that she needed to start living the life a little more. Not BASE jumping, of course. She wasn't nuts. But she needed to expand her horizons and she was doing just that. "I need to stop hiding behind books, though—for a while anyway."

Mitch rolled his head against the pillow, meeting her gaze, looking uncharacteristically introspective. "It had to be hard being the perfect kid in the family. The one who didn't get into trouble."

For a moment Ella just stared at him. "You know that was hard?" She'd never thought anyone understood.

"Of course. And we were all so glad to have someone perfect for Mom and Dad to be proud of that we let you take the bullet for us. We encouraged you to be perfect, so we didn't have to be." He relaxed back against the pillows. "Kind of shitty of us."

"I'm going to go out on a limb and guess that you didn't consciously know that you were doing that."

"Maybe not—or if we did, we didn't realize it was unfair. If it makes you feel better, we were proud as hell of you, too. But I see now that..." He grimaced as he tried to come up with the words, then abandoned mission and instead reached out and took her hand. "Elle. Like I said, I'm glad you're taking some time off. Just...don't go nuts, okay?"

"Hey," she said softly. "It's me. I'm collecting data, getting the information I need to write my grant. I might be having fun, but I'm working, too."

Mitch closed his eyes. "Good. Now I can stop worrying about you."

Chapter Four

BY THE TIME Ella pulled into Plains, Montana, she was spent. Three days on the family ranch, catching up with her siblings and parents, enjoying her father's cooking and her brother Joe's homemade red wine, left her feeling satisfied in some respects, irritated in others. She loved her family, was happy to be with them, but by the time she'd gone to bed that first night at home, she was beginning to suspect that there were two sets of standards in her family. One for her and one for everyone else. When she left she was certain of it.

Nobody came right out and said it, and Ella certainly didn't accuse anyone of thinking it, in the name of peace in the family, but by the time she packed her truck, it was crystal clear that her family seemed to think that she was a snowflake who couldn't handle life without a carved-in-stone path. They were freaking because she wasn't going back to school and didn't have a set plan for the next several months.

That was annoying.

Just because she'd always had a well-thought-out plan to

follow, it didn't mean she couldn't survive without one. Or that she couldn't give in to impulse. In fact, it was beginning to feel like she needed to prove that she could—to herself more than to her family. Any doubts she'd had about following the rodeo circuit and stepping out of her comfort zone for a few months had evaporated by the time she waved goodbye to her parents and siblings.

If anything, she hadn't been going at it hard enough.

She was no snowflake and it was high time she stopped giving people the impression that she was. If her family, who knew her better than most, had no faith in her, then she had a long way to go.

She'd made a start when she'd decided to follow the circuit with Avery, but now she needed to amp things up. She wouldn't drop her research, because she planned to return to her chosen path, but she was going to enjoy her detour, and that was why she was in Plains instead of traveling across the state to hook up with Avery in South Dakota. She had a bronc rider to interview and she had every intention of following through. Now all she had to do was find him.

The contestants were warming up in the arena when she found parking in the competitors' area, having explained to the guy guarding the entrance against people who wanted to slip into the rodeo without paying, that she was traveling with the circuit, doing research. The guy gave her a bemused look, but waved her on through.

She didn't know which truck Shane's was, so she parked

in the first available space, between two Featherlite trailers, and headed for the chutes. She wouldn't be allowed behind them, but she figured that the best place to hunt bronc riders was near the broncs.

"You can't watch from here," an official-looking guy told her as she approached the rail to the arena.

Ella's stomach tightened, as it always did when she broke rules, even by accident, but she managed a smile. "I'm actually looking for someone. Shane Marvell. I'm going to interview him after his ride."

The guy cocked his eyebrow in a way that made her think he'd heard similar stories before, but Ella maintained her cool expression. She was telling the truth and this guy could think whatever he liked.

"Then maybe you should wait by his rig."

"I don't know which rig is his."

The man gave her a that's-not-my-problem look and Ella took a backward step, gripping the shoulder strap of her messenger bag. He was only doing his job, and for all she knew, some of the competitors might have groupies or stalkers—so honestly? This guy shouldn't be helping her out.

"I understand," she said. "Thank you."

Apparently her sincerity came through, because the guy's expression relaxed an iota as he gave her a dismissive nod. She headed back toward her truck, hoping to run into T.J. or Davy Mateus, but didn't see anyone she knew. Behind her she could hear the activity in the chutes. Most of the broncs would be rigged by now. Once upon a time she'd helped Mitch with his rigging, which led to Shane remembering her hat.

Ella let out a small snort.

Her hat was in the truck, but maybe she should get it so that he recognized her. If she didn't find him after his ride, he might pull out, head back to his family ranch. How did his ranch compare to hers?

She'd have to ask.

"Hey! Interview lady!"

Startled, Ella turned to see a lanky cowboy with a redhead tucked under one arm. His free arm was in a sling.

"Hi." She'd seen him before, but didn't know his name. The redhead glowered at her, making Ella wonder if she'd accidentally insulted the woman at some point.

"Are you looking for anyone in particular?" the cowboy asked as he wheeled the redhead a few steps closer.

"I'm trying to catch up with Shane Marvell."

"That's his truck there." He pointed to a green and gray two-tone Ford. "He's up second tonight, so he should be back in short order."

Excellent, even if it did make her pulse bump at the prospect of seeing him so soon.

"Is that injury new?" she asked, nodding at his arm.

He smiled and the redhead's unfriendly expression intensified. "I had a rough go last night. But I should be okay in two weeks, which means I'll miss Dillon, but can make Red

Rock."

"You don't have to give her your schedule," the redhead muttered in a low voice that Ella may or may not have been expected to hear.

"I'm Ella, by the way," she said to the woman, smiling her friendliest smile, more to make a point than because she was feeling friendly. "I'm interviewing—"

"I know what you're doing."

"I'm Tyson. This is Sharla," the cowboy quickly interjected, frowning down at his companion.

"Nice to meet you," Sharla said in a tight voice.

Tyson sucked in a breath before giving Ella an apologetic smile. "And…we need to get going."

Ella couldn't say she'd be sorry to see them go—or rather to see Sharla go. The woman was drop-dead gorgeous and totally unpleasant. But Ella was thankful that Tyson had pointed out Shane's truck so she didn't miss him.

A cheer went up from the crowd as the first bronc rider came out of the chute and that was when Ella spotted the picnic table. She stood on the bench, which allowed her to see over the gate into the arena. The cowboy rode hard and was just coming off when the buzzer sounded.

"By golly, he made it, folks!" the announcer informed the crowd, who were hooting and clapping. "And with a score of sixty-eight points, he leads the pack. Next up, chute number four, Shane Marvell on Cracker Jack. Now this cowboy hails from the Marietta area, and he's currently number one in the standings. Let's show him some enthusiasm, folks."

The crowd complied, cheering as the gate opened and Shane's bronc turned out to the left. Watching the man buck was like watching a precision machine in operation. His neck roll touched the horse's rump and his feet moved with a rhythm that spoke of years of practice. The guy was so damned good—no wonder he was leading in the standings.

She just hoped that he didn't mind being ambushed after his ride. She didn't need to talk to him tonight, but she'd like to make arrangements to talk later. Talk and see what came out of it…and she wasn't only thinking research. Not the academic kind anyway.

The buzzer sounded and Shane took a double grip, moving his elbow sharply to the side to release his glove. The bronc moved into a corner and the pickup man hung back, waiting for the mare to move along the rail before attempting a pickup. But the mare didn't move out of the corner. She bucked and twisted and slammed Shane into the rail. Ella gasped, pressing a hand to her chest, then she exhaled slowly as the mare shot out of the corner, and Shane managed to grab the pickup man on the way by, dismounting the bronc before she raced out the gate.

A cheer went up as Shane waved his hat at the crowd. But the limp he'd had the week before was massively more pronounced. Ella had the feeling that it was only pride and adrenaline that kept him moving across the dirt toward the rails.

Slowly she climbed down from the bench and sat where she'd stood.

A lot of times it wasn't the ride, but the dismount that got a guy, which was what had happened with Mitch. He'd made his time, then bailed from the horse, only to get nailed by a flying hoof before he hit the ground. It had been a fluke, and logically Ella knew it. And she knew the chances these guys willingly took, but that didn't make it any easier to watch when they got hurt.

She stayed seated on the bench, knowing that after he collected his rigging, Shane would have to pass her on his way back to his truck. She should have worn her hat, but it was too late to go back to her truck, so she sat where she was and waited for the guy she'd driven eleven hours to reconnect with.

~

SHANE COULD FEEL his knee swelling as he walked back to his truck, Barstow rigging in one hand, his gear bag in the other. He hadn't bothered taking off his chaps, but he'd released the straps behind his thighs, so they flapped with every painful step. But, hey, unless someone had a tremendous ride, he pretty much had this rodeo sewn up with an eighty-eight. Even Boone hadn't come close.

And that was what it was about. Earning that bonus.

Hell, he used to do this for the glory. Now he had a concrete reason to endure the pain.

He hoped this knee wasn't going to give him shit for the rest of the season. He hated riding with a brace because it affected his rhythm. But if he had to, he had to. Right now, he simply wanted to make it to the truck before the joint gave out. It actually hurt bad enough to take his mind off his shoulder.

"Hey."

The softly spoken word from behind startled him. His gaze whipped around and then he blinked when he caught sight of Ella Etch standing next to a picnic table, her hands jammed into her back pockets as if she didn't quite know what to do with them.

"Ella." He felt his throat move as he swallowed. His usual cool had abandoned him, and for a second, he felt a lot like he had at junior high dances before he'd had his growth spurt and finally grew to be taller than most of the girls in his class. "I thought you were in Nevada."

"I was. But everything's okay now and I'm back." She lifted her shoulders and let them fall again in a gesture that belied the cool confidence of her facial expression. "I wanted to make new arrangements for an interview, if you're still game."

Oh, yeah. He was game.

"It doesn't have to be here," she said with a quick glance at his knee. "I'd be fine meeting up in Dillon—if you're going to Dillon that is. Avery and Jenna live close, so I'll be there."

"I'm going to Dillon." His knee was throbbing, and he shifted his weight ever so slightly as he adjusted his grip on his gear bag.

"You're about to fall over, aren't you?"

His eyebrows came together. "Why do you say that?"

"Your teeth are gritted, and your eyes are starting to cross."

"Bull." He said the word pleasantly, but even though his eyes weren't crossing, he wanted to get ice on his knee.

"Tell you what. You go to your truck and untape, and I'll go to the concession stand and get you a bag of ice."

He was about to ask if she read minds or something, then recalled that she'd been behind the chutes with her brother. "Yeah. Thanks."

She gave a brisk nod, and with her hands still in her back pockets, she turned toward the path to the concessions. Shane bit his lip against the pain and limped to his truck and horse trailer—the one with the living quarters that his brother Zach didn't let anyone borrow. But Zach seemed impressed by Shane's determination to win the Gilmore Bonus and had actually offered the use of the trailer. It was a hell of a lot more comfortable than sleeping in the back of his truck, as he tended to do on shorter trips. Plains was six hours from the ranch, so he appreciated being able to stretch out in a real bed and to wash up in the morning.

He pulled the key out from the place where he secreted it

under the wheel well of the truck and unlocked the trailer door. Then he groaned as he eased himself down until he was sitting in the open doorway instead of actually going inside. He sucked in a long breath as he experimentally straightened his knee, then bent it a little. Bone crunched on bone, but that wasn't unusual, since this was the knee where he'd done a number on the cartilage. Other than swelling and throbbing, there didn't appear to be any structural damage.

Just let me get through the season.

He straightened his knee again, sucking in another breath against the pain, then looked up at the sound of footsteps on gravel. Ella was already back with a bag full of ice.

She handed it to him as he awkwardly got to his feet. "Thanks. Give me a few minutes and I'll clean up and then we can talk."

"It doesn't have to be tonight," she reiterated.

"Let's make it tonight. Say, twenty minutes?" He had a few questions of his own, things he'd wondered about after she'd done her disappearing act.

"I'll go grab a couple burgers if you're hungry and be back in twenty. We can sit at my picnic table and keep tabs on the rodeo and talk at the same time."

"Sounds good. Let me get my wallet." Even though it was going to hurt like hell retrieving it from its hidey-hole in the trailer.

"My treat," Ella said.

"In that case, I'll meet you at the picnic table in twenty minutes."

She smiled her agreement and instantly turned and walked toward the concession area. Shane didn't know if she purposely left before he attempted to force his knee to support him as he awkwardly made his way into the trailer, or whether it had been a happy accident, but either way he was appreciative.

Once he'd made it up the step, he glanced over his shoulder, but she'd already disappeared behind the nearest trailer.

Being near her was just as distracting as he remembered. And she was here in Plains, when she was supposed to be in either Nevada or South Dakota.

The big question was, what was he going to do about it?

ELLA SAT AT the picnic table, her elbows parked on the worn wood, her hands loosely clasped in front of her face, telling herself she had no need to be nervous. But she didn't seem to be listening. Showing up in Plains, when she'd specifically told Shane that she wouldn't be going there, sent a big unspoken message.

And that message was…?

That she was her own person, and she could do as she damn well pleased. Yeah. And if he took that as a sign that she was interested in him, as opposed to picking up her research where she'd left off before Mitch's accident, well, he was right. She was interested.

She didn't yet know what she was going to do about it, and that was where the questions came in. Nice innocuous questions, which would allow her to relax. And to get to know him. Perfect plan.

But the perfect plan felt as if it could easily develop some holes when Shane appeared from behind a trailer and started toward her table. In addition to the limp, he held his arm close to his abs, speaking of some kind of an upper body injury.

Oh yeah. He was hurting. Ella totally recognized the signs from her brother's rodeo days. The thing was that her brother had been in his late teens and early twenties when he'd rodeoed and Shane was approaching his upper twenties. Bodies tended to rebel after a certain age. They didn't heal as rapidly or bounce back as quickly.

But despite the limp, he moved in a way that made it difficult to look away. Not that she wanted to. The guy was sexy as hell, but eating him up with her eyes didn't seem like a very professional way to begin an interview. He was almost to the table when she saw that he was carrying a bottle of red wine with two clear plastic glasses riding on the neck.

Really?

"I don't usually drink during an interview," she noted.

He slid onto the bench opposite her, setting the bottle

and glasses on the weathered planks that made up the top of the table. "You don't usually interview bronc riders, either."

She smiled a little. "Well, don't tell the bull riders about the wine, or they'll all expect some."

His lips twitched as he twisted the cap off. "I miss corks."

"But isn't this easier?" she asked as he poured two healthy glasses of red blend. Was he trying to deal with the pain? Or being social? Either way, she was in.

"I thought you might fight me on the wine." He set the half-empty bottle back on the table.

"Show me a Basquo who turns down wine." She'd been drinking homemade red wine with dinner since she was a kid, and during the summer her go-to drink was *kalimotxo*, wine and cola over ice, which had made Avery sneer until she tried it. Now it was also Avery's go-to summer drink.

"To tell you the truth, I don't know that many Basque. As in, none."

She lifted the plastic glass and touched it to his. "Perhaps we will remedy that."

Damn. Had she just said that?

"Is everything okay with your family?"

Ella moistened her lips. "Yes. My brother Mitch—"

"The bronc rider."

"Yes. He's the volunteer fire chief. He got injured at a fire, but it wasn't life-threatening. He's out of the hospital and at home. All is well."

"Did you know the injury wasn't life-threatening when

you took off last Saturday?"

"I did," Ella admitted, "but our family comes together in times like those. And, well, Mitch almost died a couple of years ago, so it was almost as if..." She hesitated, trying to find the best words to describe why she'd needed to make her way home.

"You had to see him with your own two eyes to make sure he was all right?"

Ella blinked at him. "Yes." Although she'd never thought of it that way.

Shane swirled his wine. Neither of them had yet taken a drink, but Ella felt better with something in her hands. "My dad had a serious accident when I was young. I remember having that reaction." One corner of his mouth tightened. "Then he had another accident and died from it." Shane met her gaze dead-on. "I guess that's why it's good to see people when you can."

Ella felt as if her breath had frozen in her chest. That was exactly how she'd felt. She'd needed to see with her own two eyes that he was okay, and she needed to see him while she could.

"I...uh..." Can't find words. Finally she said, "My family has given me a lot of worry time. They're the kind of people who tend to act without thinking, and that leads to risk taking."

"Are you like the rest of your family?"

"No." She hadn't meant for the word to come out so

quickly.

"I didn't think so."

She tilted her head and her braid slid over her shoulder. Impatiently she pushed it back where it belonged. "Why?"

"You appear to be a person who counts the cost."

"How would you know that?"

"It's a guess," he said candidly. "Or maybe intuition. A worrier usually isn't a risk-taker."

Ella picked up her wine and took a drink. It wasn't bad. Not as good as Joe's, but not bad. "I'm trying to fix that."

"How?"

"I," she said from over the top of the glass, "am doing things differently than I used to." He didn't need to know any more than that. She didn't feel like she knew him well enough to tell him more than that. Because what if her instincts were wrong? What if he wasn't the kind of guy her gut told her he was?

His gorgeous mouth curved ever so slightly. "Does that explain the near kiss outside the bar?"

The memory sent a plume of heat curling through her midsection. "Yes," she said simply. Sometimes it made no sense to hedge. Shane smiled a little and she narrowed her eyes. "What?"

"I was just thinking about vitals." He gave her a look that had her shifting in her seat.

She cleared her throat. "Maybe we should talk about risk."

"I thought we were."

"Let's shift the focus to you."

He spread his palms. "Fire away."

Chapter Five

OH, SHE'D FIRE all right. But this interview already felt different than her previous ones with the bull riders, and she had no difficulty pinpointing that difference. She wanted more from Shane Marvell than an interview. Would she get more? She had no idea, but she was ready to take a few chances instead of holding back and hoping good things came her way. A good thing sat directly in front of her.

"First of all, your answers will be private. I'm only gathering preliminary information. Once I analyze that, I'll try to shape a hypothesis and then call certain individuals for follow-up interviews and questionnaires."

"Do I need to sign something?" There was an ironic note to his voice.

"You will if I call you for more information."

"Are you going to do that?"

She allowed herself both a smile and a sip of wine. "That all depends on your answers now."

"I never was good in test situations."

"This isn't a test." Ella felt heat start the creep into her cheeks. "I just want candid answers. There is no right or wrong."

Shane gave a nod, his blue eyes looking almost silver in the glow of the pole lamp nearby, and Ella pulled the pencil out from behind her ear. Shane's lips twitched, but he didn't say a word. And she did not explain her habit.

She took down his name and age and phone number. He was twenty-six, closer to her age than she'd first thought. Not that it mattered. Nope. Didn't matter at all. She settled into scientist mode to get her mind back where it belonged.

"There are several theories as to why some people thrive on risk and others don't."

"Like…?"

She met his eyes, something she rather enjoyed doing. She'd thought about him a lot over the past week and now it was kind of surreal to actually be with him. "I'd rather not say, because I don't want to affect your answers. You are, of course, free to look them up, but I prefer not to focus on any one theory at the moment, but to just ask casual questions and listen to answers."

"Do you take notes?"

"Sometimes yes, sometimes no."

"With me?"

"I haven't decided yet." There were many things she couldn't decide about him…like why she was so drawn to him. Why she'd thought about him so much. Okay, he *was* kind of like sex incarnate with that hard body and gorgeous face, but she'd never been about casual sex.

Always a first time.

Ella cleared her throat as she once again brought her attention back to the matter at hand and Shane's eyebrows lifted as though he was aware of the direction of her thoughts.

Your thoughts are legit. You will not *blush.*

Ella steepled her fingers, trying to look as if she was thinking only about the questions she was going to ask and the answers he might give. "If I ask you about certain things, please don't give me the answer you think I want to hear. Or the macho answer."

"Like a rodeo rider would give a macho answer."

She smiled a little. "Well, you know. On the off chance."

Shane moved his knee to a different position and Ella automatically asked, "Would you be more comfortable some place different?"

He gave his head a rueful shake. "I don't think it'd matter where I was."

"How badly hurt are you?"

"Is that one of the questions?"

"It's *a* question."

He idly rubbed the shoulder he favored. "I don't focus on my injuries. They're part of the life."

A macho cowboy answer, but Ella didn't call him on it, because she knew he meant every word.

"What's the worst injury you've ridden with?" Not her

usual sequence of questions, but she could get to the basics later.

He made a face, screwing his eyes up as he searched his memory, but still looking hot as hell. "Kind of a laundry list there."

"Nothing jumps out?"

"You know, usually it's a lot of little things, coming together, which cause a change of form. And because the form is changed, it stresses parts of your body that aren't ordinarily stressed, which leads to new injuries." He dropped his hand from his shoulder. "But you already know that."

"Yes. I'm familiar, both from studies and from living with my brothers."

"Were both bronc riders?"

"As you know Mitch was, but Joseba—Joe—was a steer wrestler until he blew out his shoulder. Then he became a rock climber. It was part of his rehab, but he got addicted and now he free-climbs." Ella gave an involuntary shudder, then her eyes widened as she realized what she'd done.

"You don't like that?"

"I'm afraid of heights." Which was a totally legitimate fear and one that she had no desire to overcome. Sane people kept their feet on the ground. They did not climb rocks or jump from bridges. She picked up her pencil and returned to the safety of the canned questions. "Obviously riding rough stock is a risk. Do you take risks in other areas of your life?"

"Such as?"

"Authority defiance. Drug use. Financial risks."

His expression shifted when she mentioned finances and Ella made a mental note.

"I've had a few run-ins with authority figures. My brother, Zach, for one, as well as the occasional deputy, but that was all in good fun. Drugs…no. Alcohol? I've had my moments, but I'm pretty much in control. As to finances, I've never had enough money to take risks."

"Isn't that itself a risk?"

One corner of Shane's mouth tightened as he lightly tapped his forefinger on the wooden tabletop. He obviously didn't like the subject of finances. "I could have planned better."

And that was the end of his answer. She'd hit a nerve.

"Let me ask you this, and once again, please don't give me the answer you think I want to hear. If you won a decent jackpot in Vegas, would you cash out? Or continue to gamble, in hopes of hitting another?"

Shane leaned forward, even though it looked like the move cost him, his expression intent as he said, "A year or two ago, I would have continued gambling. Right now, I'd cash out."

"Why?"

"Because this is my last season and I need the money."

"For?"

His eyelids dropped as his chin lifted and Ella realized she'd crossed another line. Finances were an issue.

"I forgot to mention. Some questions might get personal. I may ask, but you are in no way obligated to answer. And…" she moistened her lips, her insides warming as his gaze followed the action of her tongue "…I apologize for that last question."

"You don't have to apologize. I can hold my own. I don't have an answer to that question. Just a half-baked plan, so it's not an area I want to talk about."

"Another personal question," Ella warned. "Have you ever been diagnosed with dyslexia, ADD or ADHD?"

"Attention deficit?" He leaned back as he considered, then his gaze connected with hers. "When I'm interested in something, it gets my full attention for an extended period of time."

Ella's lips parted. Did he mean…?

Or was her mind so far in the gutter that it just *seemed* like he was talking about sex? His expression bordered on innocent, but she was pretty sure she could read amusement in his eyes. "I'd like to test that sometime."

The look on his face had her fighting to hold back a smile. *Touché, Mr. Marvell.*

She glanced back at her notes, even though she knew exactly what she was going to ask. "Would you lie to someone to achieve an important personal goal, even if there was a chance they would discover the lie?"

"That would depend on the lie, I guess. And the goal."

Ella made a note, then looked up at him. "Have you

done that?"

"Yes."

"Did you get caught?"

"Yes."

"Did that change your actions in the future?"

"I still said I wasn't injured when I was, so no."

Another note. "Is that the only instance?"

A half-smile teased the corners of his mouth. "Pass."

Fair enough. Ella decided that she, too, would pass instead of asking questions on the next risk domain. She'd wait for another interview before asking if he practiced safe sex. It was not something she wanted to get into at the moment. Later, when she had a better handle on things, but right now, after driving a zillion hours to hook up with a guy she didn't know, on impulse no less…she'd wait until she was better rested.

A silence fell between them as Ella studied her notepad, then reached for her wine. Neither of them had made much headway.

"Tell me what you're doing differently in life."

Ella glanced up at the unexpected question. Before she could answer, Shane said, "I may ask personal questions, but you are under no obligation to answer."

A corner of Ella's mouth quirked. "Thanks," she said dryly.

"I'm curious." He rubbed his shoulder again, and Ella wondered if he was even aware he was doing so. "I'm making a few changes myself."

"Such as?" She took the opportunity to slide back into the driver's seat.

"Like I said, this is my last rodeo season."

"That is a change. I can assure you, however, that you will survive the transition."

"I'll miss it."

"Any idea what you'll do to replace it?"

"You mean in regard to taking risks in life?"

"No." She hadn't. She'd honestly like to know what his plans were.

"Why is it," he asked slowly, "that my questions get cleverly sidestepped?"

"I guess I'm just better at redirection. I can give you some tips, as long as you don't use them on me."

Shane laughed, then glanced down at his shirt pocket as his phone buzzed inside. He dug it out, read the text, then let out a breath. When he looked up at Ella there was genuine regret in his expression. "I gotta go."

"An emergency?"

"One of my friends has just forcibly been brought to his senses. I need to rescue him." Ella lifted her eyebrows and Shane explained, "He's been abandoned on a country road. I need to unhook the trailer and go get him."

"Ah." Ella gave a quick nod, then pushed aside her glass of wine. "Or, if you want, you could take my truck and avoid unhitching. I can watch the rodeo or wait at your trailer." When Shane sent her a questioning look, she added, "It might be that your friend in need of rescue doesn't care to have a witness to his plight."

"I think my friend deserves a witness to his plight. And I can't drive a standard transmission until the swelling goes down in my knee."

"In that case..." Ella flopped her notebook closed and slid the pencil back behind her ear "...I'd be happy to come with you."

ELLA HAD BARELY touched her wine while they'd talked, so she poured out almost an entire glass before she and Shane headed toward her truck. Probably a good thing she hadn't imbibed, since she was driving. Shane tried not to limp too badly on his way to her truck, then gave it up and put a hand on her shoulder. She shot him a quick look and he came clean.

"I'm breaking the bronc rider's machismo creed, but I need to get some ice on this knee again, and I need a little help getting to your truck."

Her mouth opened, then closed again, as if she was afraid of spooking him back into macho territory by saying something. Instead she nodded, which made him feel ridiculously warm inside. She got it. She knew that asking for help was a big deal to him, and she didn't make anything of it.

His kind of woman.

The thought floored him.

No. More like the kind of woman with qualities he could appreciate.

"Do you think the three of us can fit in here?" she asked as she stopped next to a very small four-wheel-drive truck. He gave her a dubious look. "I don't need a lot of room since I usually travel alone, in case I'm going somewhere Avery and Jenna are not."

Like Plains, Montana?

"I figured. Bench seat? We can fit."

Unfortunately, due to his knee, he wouldn't have the middle. While Tyson deserved to be scrunched between them, Shane couldn't say he was wild about the idea of his friend's thigh being pressed against Ella's.

The rodeo was just ending as they pulled out of the competitors' area, and they were caught up in rodeo gridlock for a good fifteen minutes before they finally hit the open road.

"And we're going…?"

"North. We turn off at a place with two silos and then follow a gravel road."

"Off the pavement. Hmm. Sounds like your friend got himself into a jam."

Shane gave a small snort. "Yeah. Like four months ago." Ella shot him a look and he explained, "Bad choice of companions. She's easy on the eyes, but really controlling."

"Redhead?" Ella asked.

"Yeah," he replied on a note of surprise.

"A guy named Tyson told me which truck yours was earlier this evening."

"A guy named Tyson is now stranded on the mountain because his girlfriend abandoned him. He must have given the wrong answer to some question."

"I can see that happening," Ella said in a way that made him think that she'd seen Sharla in action.

"There're the silos." Shane pointed to a well-lit farm just off the main road. "We turn just after them."

Ella slowed and made the turn. They passed the farm and almost immediately came to a fork. One road was gravel, the other barely a track, so Ella followed the more traveled road. A mile later the gravel disappeared and the road started to get bumpy. And steep. They climbed for another mile, the bad feeling Shane had gotten when the gravel disappeared intensifying as they drove.

What in the hell had Tyson and Sharla been doing out here?

What if they hadn't been out here at all?

Shane glanced over at Ella after she drove around a rut. "Do you think there could have been more than one set of silos on the highway?"

"I'm beginning to believe that, yes."

The problem was that the road was narrow and they were now in a place with high banks on one side and a pretty good drop-off on the other.

"I hope we don't have to go to the top of the mountain before we can turn around."

"I don't think the road will take us that far."

Indeed, it was deteriorating rapidly. "It's going to be hell to get back down the road." Especially after she'd maneuvered tightly around some of the deep ruts. They might not be so lucky repeating the maneuvers in reverse.

He was about to offer to drive, despite his knee, when she said, "I can turn around."

The cool confidence of her reply made him frown at her. "Yeah?" He could probably turn around here, too, but he'd grown up on roads like these.

"Just as soon as I find the right spot."

They rounded a corner and Ella slowed to a stop in front of a wind-fallen tree. "This is the spot."

Shane didn't think so. The incline of the road wasn't bad, but the drop-off to the gully on their left was treacherous.

As if sensing his thoughts, Ella turned the steering wheel and moved a foot toward the gully until the bumper nudged the tree, leaving them at an angle in the road. And it wasn't a very good angle. She put the truck in reverse, turned to look out the back window and moved until she'd put her rear bumper firmly into the bank, then spun the wheels a little for good measure.

Really?

She went forward again, this time the front bumper

touching the tree in a different spot, a few inches closer to the gully. Back she went, into the bank, cranking the wheel hard.

Shane hadn't realized he was hanging on to the oh-shit handle above his door until she'd made five more short forward and reverse passes. When the front tires came to the very edge of the road, bumping a rock down the gully, he sucked a breath in through his teeth. Ella coolly put the truck in reverse and backed up to safety.

On the next forward swing after that, she managed a complete one eighty.

Shane let go of his death grip on the handle and shot her a look. She was smiling.

"See? I do this all the time when we gather the cows in the mountains."

It took him a moment to say, "I thought you were the sane one in your family."

She laughed lowly, then started back down the rutted road. "There are risks, Shane. And then there are risks."

He had no idea what that meant, other than she was pretty damned good at getting a truck out of a tight spot.

"We could have backed down."

"Uh-uh. The chances of success are slim. The rear tires would have slid into a rut. Listen to one who speaks from experience."

"You must run your cattle in rough country."

"Yes."

The simple answer told him what a lot of explanation couldn't have. Ella might be the cautious one in her family, but she was no pansy. He hadn't thought she was, but now he had solid evidence.

By the time they made it back to the main road, Shane's hand was beginning to uncramp from where he'd grabbed the safety strap so tightly. He was glad she didn't notice, because hey…he didn't want to look like a pussy in front of a woman he was trying to impress. A woman who'd done a good job of impressing him.

He couldn't help casting the occasional glance Ella's way and admiring the coolness with which she'd handled the situation. And she hadn't said one word about taking the wrong road. It was as if she was very used to that kind of thing, and from the hints she'd dropped about her family, maybe she was.

"Hey," she said, taking her hand off the wheel to point. "There are two more silos."

Sure enough.

"I'm going to have to talk to Tyson about his directions," Shane muttered as Ella turned onto the road, which was in much better shape than the one they'd just traveled.

They didn't have to drive far before the headlights shone on a lone figure walking down the center of the road, one arm in a sling.

He raised a hand and waved as Ella slowed down.

"Does he think we'll miss him?" Ella asked, a smile in her

voice.

"No. He's just grateful." Or he'd better be. "And probably wondering what the hell took us so long."

She pulled to a stop and Shane eased his way out of the truck, giving a small grunt of pain, and he maneuvered his knee out and his foot onto the ground.

"What took you so long?" Tyson asked.

"Long story." Shane wasn't going to hit a guy when he was down by complaining about his inability to count silos, and Tyson looked borderline pathetic, his arm in the sling, his hat pushed back on a sweat-beaded forehead, making Shane wonder if he'd been running. Never a lot of fun with a cast. "You're damned lucky you had a cellular signal here."

"Actually I had a pretty healthy walk to a signal," Tyson said before leaning down to squint into the cab. "Who did you bring to witness my humiliation?"

"Hi," Ella said, lifting a hand in greeting.

"Guess you found his truck," Tyson said, standing up again and drilling Shane with a look. "The mystery is, why didn't you guys bring that truck?"

"I didn't want to unhitch the trailer." Or operate a clutch.

Tyson gave his head a shake, then folded his body down into the cramped center seat, his knees close to his chest after he was finally situated. "No more than I deserve," he muttered as Shane climbed in and made two attempts to close the door before he got the job done.

"It's like living in Avery's trailer," Ella murmured before putting the truck in gear. She had to reach between Tyson's boots to do so.

"Maybe you should have unhitched the trailer," Tyson said, leaning his head against the rear window.

"I'm not going to ask what led to you being out here without your truck."

"Because you know I'm going to tell you. Sharla got pissed." He didn't seem at all shy about talking in front of Ella.

"Did you look twice at some girl at the rodeo?"

"More like a lot of little things started piling up. We went for a drive to discuss them and ended up with her locking me out of the truck and driving off. I have no idea how I'm supposed to get my truck back, unless she comes back for round two."

"I think you should call the deputies on her."

Tyson turned his head, bringing his face uncomfortably close to Shane's. "You dislike her that much?"

"You want the truth or a lie?"

Tyson looked toward the windshield again. "I always did have to learn things the hard way."

Shane hoped the lesson took and Sharla didn't talk his friend into taking her back—but he could see it happening.

"She's got control issues, Tyson." And his friend liked to rescue and rehabilitate. He undoubtedly saw something redeemable in Sharla—something invisible to Shane.

"I guess. I thought if I was patient…" He let the sentence hang. "Thanks for coming to get me, you guys."

"Not a problem," Ella said, sounding utterly sincere, almost as if she'd enjoyed the adventure.

"Can I crash in your trailer until I find my truck?" Tyson asked Shane.

"Sure. Ella, you can, too, if you want."

"I have a room."

"I think I'll stay with Ella," Tyson said. He glanced toward her. "Two beds?" he asked hopefully.

"No," Shane said matter-of-factly. "I think you'll sleep in my trailer."

Chapter Six

AFTER TALKING ALL the way back to town, Tyson fell silent when Ella dropped them off at the rodeo grounds before heading to her motel room. He'd been amazingly open about his problems with Sharla, had told Ella about the side of Sharla most people didn't see—the side he enjoyed being with. The side that Shane thought was a figment of his friend's imagination. And Ella listened sympathetically.

Shane had sat in silence, because it was obvious that his friend wanted a woman's point of view, not that of a guy who wanted to call the deputies. Honestly? Tyson was too nice for his own good. And people like Sharla took advantage.

By the time they reached the rodeo grounds, Ella and Tyson were talking like old friends, and Shane felt something that smacked of jealousy. Not the green-eyed, hot-blooded kind, but rather the why-him-and-not-me kind.

Why did he feel so damned possessive of this woman's time? Even though he was glad that he'd been able to come to Tyson's rescue and hopeful that Sharla's latest stunt had opened his friend's eyes for good, he really wished he'd been able to spend the evening with Ella. Alone.

After getting into their respective bunks, Shane on the fold-out bed next to the dining table since he didn't feel up to climbing into the larger bed over the nose of the trailer that Tyson was now occupying, the two men lay in silence, staring at the ceiling, dealing with their respective issues. Shane finally rolled over onto his uninjured side, dragging the light blanket over him. A second later a light tap sounded on the door, startling him.

"I'll get it," Tyson muttered, climbing down out of the bed and landing on his feet with a gentle thud. "I walk better than you."

"It better not be T.J.," Shane muttered.

Tyson crossed the three-foot distance to the door and cracked it to see who was out there, before pulling it all the way open, letting a rush of cool air into the small interior.

"They gave away my motel room."

The sound of Ella's voice brought Shane up onto his good elbow. Really?

"I assume your offer stands?" she asked in a low voice, as if afraid of waking the neighbors.

"Of course." Tyson, who was in his boxers, moved back and Ella stepped into the trailer, closing the door behind her.

"Sorry about this. My truck is too small to sleep in, unless I stretch out in the back, and I don't like to do that in public places."

"Probably because you're not stupid," Shane said before adding, "I'm glad you came here."

"Yeah." She dropped her bag on the bunk opposite his. "I would have figured something out, but this seemed easiest." She took the blanket Tyson handed her before he climbed back into the upper bed, and spread it on the bench where she'd be sleeping. "Who gives away motel rooms in this day and age? They said I hadn't checked in by 9:00 p.m. and that was their policy."

"Sorry about that," Shane said. If she hadn't driven him to get Tyson, she might be in a more comfortable room than the one she was now in. Of course, he would have never known about her mountain road skills if Tyson hadn't called, and he liked knowing that about her.

"Not your fault they have an archaic policy," Ella said as she pried off her boots and placed them next to his. "Most places just charge the card, but not this one."

"This is cheaper," Shane said. And the crazy thing was that having her there made him feel more relaxed, instead of more on edge. He liked knowing where she was.

No. You like having her close.

Yeah. He definitely was going to have to think about this.

Ella settled onto the cushion of the fold-out without bothering to fold it out. Maybe she felt better sleeping in a small space with two guys if she wasn't in an actual bed. A second later she kicked her jeans out from under the cover and if he wasn't mistaken, unhooked her bra.

His body stirred, and he told it to stop.

"Hey, Ella?" he murmured.

"Yeah?"

"Good job getting us down off the mountain."

She gave a low laugh as Tyson asked, "What?" in a sleepy voice.

"Never mind."

Ella laughed again, so lightly he could barely hear it, then he forced himself to roll over and face the wall.

~

SHANE AND TYSON were both snoring softly when Ella jerked awake. Judging by the light filtering in through the windows, it had to be close to dawn, so she snuggled a little deeper under the blanket, not yet ready to face the day. Or the guys she was sharing quarters with, although there was something comforting about the rhythm of their breathing. She considered grabbing her boots and jeans, which lay in a heap on the floor not that far from Shane's boots and jeans, and slipping out of the trailer.

Except slipping away seemed like a chicken-shit thing to do. Exactly what she might have done in the past to make things easier on everyone—meaning her—but not the way she wanted to part company with Shane Marvell.

He rolled over and she automatically held her breath, staining to hear if he resumed his previous breathing pattern.

He did not. She was awake. He was awake. Tyson snored on, making her feel as if they were alone in the small quarters.

Man up. So she might have dreamed about the guy—she had no specific memories, just a suspicion that they'd done the deed in her mind and that she'd enjoyed it very much—big deal. It was time to hit the road, hook up with Avery and Jenna at their place just outside of Dillon, the site of the next rodeo.

She thrust her hand out from under the blanket and fished around for her jeans, dragging them under the blanket and awkwardly working her way into them. Shane didn't say of word. Nor did he speak when she grabbed her boots and her bag and then quietly got out of bed and made her way out of the trailer, softy closing the door behind her. She wasn't running away. She'd take care of the morning necessities in the public restroom, then go back and say goodbye.

Then she'd run away.

Ella unlocked her truck, threw in her bag and reached inside to get the smaller bag with her personal items. She'd never been so much of a runner, as an avoider of trouble—because someone in the family had to take on that role. Otherwise there'd be no one on the outside to post bond.

Okay. That was a bit of an exaggeration. It was more like the situation with Shane the previous evening—someone needed to be capable of driving.

Whatever, the more time she spent *not* dodging trouble that probably wasn't going to find her anyway, the freer she felt. Returning to the trailer, spending the night with Shane and Tyson had put her in a good mood and given her the feeling that anything was possible. She'd done something that she might not have done a few months ago. More than that, she felt as if she'd made the right decision when she'd chosen to not go back to school. Some people needed a gap year after high school. She'd needed one after college graduation. Doing a double major in education and psychology had taken a lot of time and money and energy.

The air was damp and full of smells she associated with rodeo—crushed grass, wet earth, the faint aroma of animals and concessions. An odd mix, but a familiar one. She didn't rodeo herself, but heaven knew she'd been to enough of them—both as a spectator and as Mitch's backup rig-puller when his best friend was laid up or unavailable. He could have had anyone do it, or could have done it himself, but he trusted Ella and was a touch superstitious. Maybe he had a point, because every time she'd helped him out, he'd been in the points.

Ella spent some time in the bathroom washing up in cold water, smoothing her hair into a braid, giving up on the wispy tendrils around her face. She changed her clothes, slid her feet back into her boots and packed up her belongings. Avery had texted, even though it was ridiculously early, and told her that she and Jenna were on their way back to her place after spending the night in Billings. Ella would arrive in Dillon about the same time as the sisters if she stopped for breakfast and they didn't. She was starving, so she was going to stop and indulge in a waffle with whipped cream somewhere along the way.

Shane was standing between his truck and trailer, checking the trailer connections, when she started back to the parking area. She went to her truck, tossed her bag inside. Took a deep light-of-day breath.

Time to say goodbye.

She kind of hated it, but hey…life.

Shane straightened as she approached, and she noted that he didn't move toward her. His knee had to be giving him hell this morning. As was his shoulder, judging from the way he held his arm. But he smiled at her as she approached, and she smiled back.

There was something about this guy that both shook her up and gave her confidence. A heady mix.

"I'm taking off," she said.

He nodded and finally took a couple limping steps. She lifted her eyebrows but didn't say a word about the obvious or ask any questions. Yes, he was hurting, no, he was not 'all right,' but he was a rough-stock rider and he would muscle through.

"Any particular destination?"

"Avery's place. We're meeting up there."

She moved closer, stopping less than a foot away and settling her hands on her belt buckle to keep from reaching out to him. But what the heck? Why not reach out?

She let go of her buckle and raised her hand to lightly lay her palm against his unshaven cheek. His skin was warm, the stubble beneath her palm rough. Her insides began to melt down with just that one touch, and the intensity of his gaze, the question in his eyes, made her breath hitch. *Maintain, Ella.*

And maintain she would. She rose on her toes to kiss his firm lips, purposely refraining from leaning in to him as she wanted to so badly. His hand came up to capture hers, his fingers closing as he kissed her back. A long slow kiss that left her with no doubts as to whether the attraction was mutual, which in turn left her both frustrated and glad that Tyson was still asleep in the living quarters. Oh, the things she wanted to do—but was she ready? The thought irked her.

Was she *ever* going to stop second-guessing herself?

Maybe with practice.

Yes. Practice. When Shane ended the kiss, she pulled his lips to hers again for another sweet moment of exploration before gently pulling her hand free and stepping back.

"What was that for?" He smiled down at her, his eyes half closed, but watchful.

Ella had the feeling that Shane was fighting to regain his own equilibrium. Otherwise he wouldn't have asked such an obvious question. 'That' was because she thought he was the hottest thing in cowboy boots. But her saner self took over, and she left the thought unspoken. "I told you I couldn't interview you if we kissed. Interview is over."

"I don't feel as if you got the full story. We were interrupted."

"Is there more you'd like to say?"

"Yeah." His gaze narrowed thoughtfully. "Will you be at Dillon?"

"Probably."

"So will I."

"You want to see me there?"

"I'm thinking I would."

Ella gave a slow nod. "I'd like that, too. I have some other interviews lined up, but I can work you in."

"For an interview?"

She smiled a little. "Or whatever."

Shane looked as if he liked the idea of whatever. He leaned in and took her lips, kissing her like he meant it, then stepped back.

"Travel safe," he said.

Ella nodded and got into her truck. Shane stayed where he was as she started the engine and put the vehicle in gear. It felt kind of empty without two guys crammed into it next to her. She pushed her hair back from her forehead with one hand and glanced into the rearview mirror as she headed for the main road. Shane stood watching her go. What would he do if she swung the truck around and headed back?

Better question—what would she do?

She bit her lip, focused her eyes back on the road so she wouldn't hit anything.

Going to Plains had been a wise decision. One she wouldn't have made a year ago—and one she did not in the least regret.

It had been a fine adventure, and she was very curious as to what Dillon might bring.

"STAY STRONG."

They were the only words of advice Shane gave Tyson before dropping him in the parking lot of a local restaurant where he was to meet with Sharla, who'd texted while Shane had been kissing Ella.

Tyson gave him a speaking look, then reached for the door handle. His truck was parked in a space directly in front of the restaurant, its sides covered with mud. Had Sharla gone mud bogging after abandoning Tyson?

"I'll wait," Shane said.

"No." Tyson, held the door for a moment. "I'll work this out. I'm getting my truck back come hell or high water."

Shane had no doubt of that. He just hoped his friend would work it out so that Sharla wasn't messing with his life anymore. Yeah. Tyson was too nice for his own good. And like most good guys, he paid for it.

"Good luck."

Tyson nodded and closed the door. He hadn't said one word about Ella, but Shane could tell that his friend was wondering what the deal was there. So was Shane. Especially after kissing her. It'd been all he could do not to pull her close and feel the length of her body pressed against his.

He wanted more.

He sensed that he wasn't alone in that. The expression on her face as she'd looked up at him after the kiss ended—part longing, part relief to be stepping back into her safety zone—had stayed with him.

If Ella was looking for a summer adventure, then he could well be the man for the job. It might be good for both of them. Losing Darcy had shaken his confidence, but his time with Ella had started him thinking about something other than rodeo and winning, and showing people just who did and did not have a future.

He pulled to the edge of the parking lot, then sat with the engine idling as Tyson went into the restaurant, debating about staying close by just in case.

Tyson was a big boy. He could handle this.

Shane put the truck in gear and headed toward the exit. His brother Cody had texted as he and Tyson had left the rodeo grounds and asked to meet at Grey's Saloon in Marietta before Shane drove on to the ranch. He had no idea what that was about, but Marietta was only five hours away, and he could make it without stopping. His knee was killing him, and operating the clutch was murder, but he didn't have much reason to shift gears up and down if he stayed on the highways. He could hold off on a pit stop and working the clutch until Grey's. Once he got home, he had five days to rest the knee and get it back in shape for Dillon.

Where he was going to see Ella again.

Chapter Seven

"WHAT? DID YOU think I was going to melt down or something?" Shane stared at his brother over an almost full glass of beer. He'd been somewhat suspicious when Cody had asked if they could meet in town, and sure enough, Cody had dropped a bomb shortly after the beer arrived.

"Well, it's only been a few months since you asked Darcy to marry you."

"Closer to a year." Exactly eight months on August 24th, if anyone was counting.

Cody made a who-cares gesture. "You guys dated for two years, she turns you down, and then agrees to marry a guy she's only dated since spring. Way less than a year."

"Your point?" Shane asked in a deadly tone. He hated being on the receiving end of sympathy, especially when the situation was one of his own creation.

"I'm trying to help. And to explain why Cal might be kind of shifty around you."

They'd gone to high school with Cal Llewelyn, who was

their CPA. And now he was also Darcy's affianced. No matter how Shane looked at it, the situation sucked—and it also drove home the point that he had nothing to offer. Cal, on the other hand, had a business degree, a nice place with lots of room for horses—Darcy's passion—and a steady job with a healthy paycheck.

He had a future.

So will you. After this season, you'll have the resources to start building.

Shane barely listened to himself.

Darcy had seen him as a fun guy to burn time with. He'd seen her as a potential life partner.

He'd felt so stupid when she'd made it clear that she loved him, a lot, but had to think about practicalities. It still bothered the hell out of him. How was it that he hadn't thought about practicalities? He'd been so oblivious that it was embarrassing to think about. Oh yeah—he and Darcy would ride into the sunset, build a life, have lots of little kids and share a one-bathroom house with his brothers.

Right.

Shane picked up his beer, took a healthy drink because Cody would expect him to. If he didn't act normally, then his middle brother would go into his whole make-everything-right act. Cody was the peacemaker of the family, when he wasn't stirring up shit.

"I'm good with Darcy being engaged," he said after wiping foam off his mouth with the back of his hand. "If she's found the guy she wants to spend the rest of her life with, more power to her."

"Okay," Cody said, eying him sideways.

"All right." Shane gave a nod.

"Just thought you should know."

"If you try to hug me, I'll deck you."

Cody laughed and picked up his beer, but the smile didn't reach his eyes. He was worried about his little brother.

Shit.

"You aren't going to try to set me up, are you? Take my mind off Darcy and all that? Because I can take care of myself in that regard." Once Cody had tried that with their older brother, Zach, who'd been going through a rough patch, and it had been an unmitigated disaster.

"No. Learned my lesson."

"Good."

"Heard a rumor that you've been seeing someone."

Shane had been mid-drink and coughed as the beer went down the wrong pipe. His eyes were watering when he looked at his brother. "What?" he managed.

"A lady from Nevada."

"And if I am?" Who'd ratted him out? Boone? Shane sincerely doubted it. For one thing, there hadn't been time for him to get back to Marietta and run into Cody.

"I think that's a positive."

"It would be. *If* I were seeing her."

"Are you?" Cody gave him the deadeye, meaning he

wasn't going to let the matter drop, and Shane decided to come clean.

"Not yet."

Cody grinned widely. "Good to have you back."

He might be back, but he was not the same. Not even close. If he and Ella hooked up, it would be with a full understanding of what they expected from one another, now and in the future. Which sounded really serious, and kind of anal, but after Darcy, he was all about full disclosure. If Darcy had told him he was just her good-time guy, he would have tried to do something about it before it was too late—or he would have moved on. He definitely wouldn't have made plans for a shared future, only to be slapped backward.

"You're really okay with Darcy getting engaged?"

"Not totally, but it's hurt pride, not a broken heart."

"Yeah," Cody said as he pulled his wallet out of his pocket to pay for the round. "It's good to have you back."

"Cool. Now if you don't mind explaining, why are you telling me the happy news here instead of at home?"

Cody's gaze shifted. "Because Cal is at the ranch going over some business stuff with Zach. He should be gone by the time we get there, but…"

"I get it. When did they get engaged?"

"Two days ago."

"I appreciate the warning." Shane drained his beer and set the mug on the table. "Let's get lunch at the café, then head home."

ELLA PUSHED HER reading glasses higher on her nose as she studied her transcribed notes. So far her questions were fairly free-form. She tried to hit all the domains of risk—financial, health, social, recreation, and ethics, in a manner that felt more like a conversation than a question and answer period. She was looking for trends, something to zero in on. Correlations to health or brain issues, home environment, genetics, role models. From there she'd create a more formal survey, which she would tackle in either the spring or summer of the following year.

She sighed and pushed her glasses to the top of her head. She *was* getting a feel for the kinds of questions that produced the most interesting answers, and she was making a list of guys she wanted to include in a more in-depth study once she'd nailed down some financing. Or gave it all up and took out yet another loan. As things were now, she'd be paying off student loans for most of her life. She didn't regret the money she'd spent...but she was not in the mood to spend more.

She should have gotten that freaking assistantship, worked on one of Dr. Bruch's projects. Gotten paid while collecting and analyzing data.

But she hadn't, which had changed her perspective, and not necessarily for the worse. Maybe she needed to focus on that. Serendipitous consequences.

Like Shane Marvell.

She wasn't certain what she was going to do about him, but after that kiss, she *was* certain that she didn't want him to slip out of her life. Not until she'd had a chance to do more exploration of character…and perhaps other things.

She leaned back in her chair and stretched. Avery and Jenna shared a small farmhouse a few miles from Dillon where Jenna attended college. Unlike their trailer, the farmhouse had three bedrooms, so Ella had her own space when she stayed with them. Since she and Avery had been college roomies, all the intricacies of sharing space had been worked out long ago, resulting in a harmonious environment that made her wish the summer could stretch on forever. It wouldn't, which meant she needed to make a plan.

But she didn't need to make it now. She'd go to the Dillon rodeo in two days, connect with a couple of local bull riders as well as a not-so-local bronc rider, and take it from there.

Talk about freedom. Mitch would be proud.

HE WASN'T READY for this ride. His knee had gotten worse rather than better during the time on the ranch—to the point that he'd used the four-wheeler to get around while riding fence more than his horse, because riding killed his knee.

Three more rodeos. Hopefully he didn't blow the joint to hell before the last one.

Shane sucked in a breath and stepped over the rail and eased himself down onto his bronc, allowing the horse time to settle before working his glove into the handle of the rigging. Tyson had ridden first and eaten dirt two seconds in. He'd stayed strong concerning Sharla, who now seemed to want him more than ever, which might have explained why his focus was off. Or maybe he'd just had a bad day.

Shane couldn't afford a bad day, and he hated that his head was not where it belonged—focused on the ride ahead instead of on other matters, such as a certain dark-haired Nevada cowgirl, whom he'd yet to see. Was she even there?

And why the hell was he thinking shit like this when it was go time?

Shane gave the nod and the gate swung open.

Lil Bee sprang into the arena with such agility that Shane almost missed marking her out. Then muscle memory settled in in a way that it hadn't during the past two rides and he was in his Zen place, going through what felt, in some regards, like a slow-motion ballet and, in others, as if he were the ball in a rather vicious handball match. The solid muscles of the mare's rear end hit his neck roll with a satisfying rhythm as his knees came up, then extended. Up. Extend.

What felt like a couple of hours later, the buzzer sounded and Shane grabbed the rigging with his free hand, pulling forward and cracking his elbow open so he could pull his glove free. The pickup man was in perfect position and Shane made a grab, dragging himself off the bronc, his bad knee hitting the horse's backbone.

The next thing he knew he was on solid ground, his feet stinging from the impact, which beat the hell out of having his shoulder or ribs stinging from impact. Sounds started to filter in: the thud of hooves, the noise of the crowd.

Sheer adrenaline got him to the gate without his knee buckling. The announcer gave the score—eighty-nine—and Shane waved his hat before the gateman let him out of the arena. A couple of guys congratulated him on his way to pick up his rigging, and he nodded and smiled.

Once he had his rigging in hand, he started toward his trailer, wanting nothing more than to get out of the tape and to slap an ice pack on his knee.

"Need some help with that?"

A familiar voice brought his head up as he cleared the chute area and a smile creased his cheeks. He felt like it'd been a year, rather than days, since he'd seen Ella.

"I've got it."

She fell into step with him, walking slowly so as not to hurry his limping gait. Shane drew in a long breath, filling his lungs, marveling at how, now that she was there, all felt right with the world.

Reality?

Or the way he wanted things to be?

"Nice ride."

Shane gave a grunt of acknowledgment and was rewarded with a shoulder nudge, which made him smile a little.

"Good macho response," Ella murmured dryly.

"I don't want to jinx myself. I have another ride tomorrow."

"How are you spending your time in between?" Ella shot him a sideways look. "Other than elevating your leg and icing your knee?"

"I…uh…thought I might ice my shoulder, too."

Ella waited until they were closer to his trailer before saying, "Maybe I could help you with that." The look Shane sent her must have startled her, because she started to backtrack. "Too forward?"

He quickly shook his head. "No. More like more than I'd hoped for."

"You had hopes?" she asked in a low voice, her gaze not quite meeting his.

"A few."

"Ah." She sounded like a scientist who'd just made a satisfying discovery. Which made him want to hear her make that sound again. Perhaps in a more intimate setting.

They stopped at the door of his trailer, then Shane took the big leap and said, "Do you want to come inside?"

He saw Ella's throat move as she swallowed. "Yes. I would."

He stepped back to allow her to enter first, then followed her in, grimacing as his knee did its best not to cooperate. He set his rigging and his chaps on top of his gear bag next to the small kitchenette unit, then reached behind him for the door handle.

"I...um..." Ella smiled nervously. "What's the deal with your shoulder?"

Not what Shane had been expecting. "Partial tear of the labrum."

"Do you tape yourself?"

"When I have to. It's awkward, but the sports guys aren't at some of the smaller rodeos." Shane's heart beat a little faster as he said, "Want to see?"

Ella sat down on the bench she'd slept on less than a week ago. "Yes."

Shane shrugged out of his protective vest, tossed it on top of the rest of his gear and unsnapped his shirt. Ella swallowed again, making him wonder if she'd spent much time with guys in intimate situations.

Or if it was a matter of her being nervous around him.

He shrugged out of his shirt and stepped closer so she could see the wrap job he'd done. She got to her feet and inspected the front, then put a light hand on his shoulder to turn him, so she could see the back, too. "How many rolls of tape on your elbow?"

"More than one. I don't want to hyperextend."

She ran an exploratory hand over the thick layers of white athletic tape covering the area from his bicep to the middle of his forearm. Then she made the mistake of glancing up. Their gazes locked and it was suddenly very clear to him what needed to be done. Ella was of the same mind. They leaned closer at the same moment, their lips meeting. Her hand tightened on his taped forearm as she welcomed his tongue into her mouth, teased it with her own. She broke contact too soon, leaving him wanting more.

Smoothing her hair from her forehead, she stepped back, putting space between them. "Just so you know, I didn't ask to see the tape job as an excuse to have my way with you."

"You can't imagine how disappointed I am." Maybe he shouldn't have said that, even if it was the truth, because he didn't want things to get out of hand before he got a handle on them.

"I thought about you a lot over the past week."

His chest tightened at her admission. "Likewise."

"We don't know each other that well."

"I feel like we do."

"That's the crazy thing. I feel like that, too. I don't know if it's a manifestation of something I haven't yet pinpointed—"

Shane's lips twitched as she began using the science lingo.

"Or rampant horniness."

The twitch became a genuine smile. "Come here."

She stepped closer, her hands sliding up his chest to his shoulders as he wrapped his arms around her, brought his lips down to meet hers. The kiss was long and slow and excellently thorough.

"I like going there," she said against his mouth. She

pressed against his erection and he went in for another long kiss, pushing his free hand into her hair, cupping the back of her head as he explored.

This was new territory for him. Did he outline some caveats? Mention that he was working toward a goal, that he wasn't in a place he wanted to be?

Or follow his gut and enjoy the moment for what it was?

He went with option B. She was the one who brought up horniness. He was the guy doing something about it. He was also the guy with a niggling of conscience. He eased back, bringing his forehead down to Ella's. They didn't need to spell out exactly what they were looking for and lay down rules and game plans, but he wasn't about to go into anything half-cocked. He liked both Ella and his peace of mind too much for that.

Ella raised those hazel eyes of hers, which were so close that he could see small flecks of gold and green, then she moistened her lips as she studied him as if trying to get a read.

"Let's go slow," he said.

She nodded against his forehead in a way that made him think she'd been having the same thoughts. The chemistry between them didn't feel as if it was going to fade anytime soon, and if it did, it hadn't been real anyway.

She ran her hands over his arms and then his shoulders, her fingertips dragging over the tape, then coming back to bare skin, sending a shiver through him. His grip automatically tightened on her waist, telegraphing the effect she had on him.

"Slow now? Or overall?"

The thought of taking it slow now, of laying her down on the bunk and exploring every inch of her with his hands, his lips and his tongue made his erection swell against the restraint of the spandex shorts he wore when he rode. "That's it," he muttered, "make it difficult."

"Not my intention."

Shane let out a breath and eased back, looking down at her. "I'm not in a good place."

"Obviously. You're taped from head to toe." Despite her flippant response, Shane had caught the flash of concern in her expression.

"I got dumped in December. I wanted to marry her, but she wasn't wild about my lifestyle." A whole lot of heartache in two sentences. Not bad.

"Am I your rebound girl?"

Shane frowned down at her, surprised at the question. And also surprised that it wasn't easy to form an answer. "You're special. And right now I don't feel worthy of special."

Something sparked in her expression that looked a whole lot like annoyance, but her tone was even as she said, "How self-sacrificing of you."

Not the answer he'd expected. "I thought it was kind of noble."

"It is," she said on a sigh. "Especially given current conditions."

She glanced down to where his hard-on was pressing against her abs, but she didn't step back. He lightly threaded his fingers through her hair on either side of her face. "What do you suggest?"

She considered for a moment. "Part of me wants to back you up to that bunk and have my way with you. Another part says that anticipation is golden."

He frowned down at her. "Are you sure you're the cautious one in your family?"

She gave a slow nod, her gaze holding his. "So you can imagine what the rest are like." She stepped back, putting a space between them and he reluctantly dropped his hands to his sides. "I'll help you with your tape," she said. "Don't worry. I will behave myself."

Shane shook his head, then turned to grab the duckbill scissors from the tiny counter next to the even tinier sink. "Have at it."

She eased the scissors under the edge of the tape and started working her way through it. Her hands skimmed over his skin, activating every nerve in his body. "Sorry. I'm having a hard time controlling myself."

Shane bit his lip to keep from laughing, but his shoulders shook a little.

"Careful. Don't want to have to give you stitches." She turned him around and started to work on the back.

Ella tackled the tape at his elbow, and there was a lot of it there. Shane closed his eyes as she expertly worked her way through it. When she was done, she turned him back around and placed her palm on the center of his chest, her gaze focused on the muscles that tightened beneath her light touch.

"I lied, Shane…" She looked up at him, the expression in her hazel eyes making his semi-erection snap back to full attention. "I'm not going to behave myself."

He swallowed. Hard. Then took her hand and moved it down his abdomen to the waistband of his jeans.

"Good."

Chapter Eight

HIS SKIN TASTED faintly of dust and salt. Arena dust and sweat to be exact, and Ella didn't care one bit. If anything, it added to the heady sensation of trailing kisses down Shane's neck.

His hands traveled over her body, lightly, not possessively. Yet. She sensed that moment would come. She returned the favor as they continued to shed clothing, exploring with lips, tongues, fingertips as they went.

Shane's body was amazing in its hard contours, bruised and beaten in some areas, an example of perfect masculinity in others. When her hands skimmed over the spandex briefs he wore, his breath caught. When her lips traced the same path, he cursed and fisted his hands in her hair.

And then she slowly rolled down the top, exposing a massive erection and her own breath caught. Oh yes. She wanted this. In the very worst way.

Or maybe she meant in the very best way.

She took him into her mouth, circled him with her tongue, reveled in the way he sucked air through his teeth.

"Ella..."

She understood the warning in his voice. Knew that if their roles were reversed and he touched her sex with his lips, she'd climax instantly. And she wasn't about instant. Not this first time.

She released his erection and stepped back, peeling her underwear down her thighs. Shane's gaze followed her hands, then, after she'd kicked them free, he took her by the waist and lifted her onto the bunk, easing his way between her open thighs. The blunt head of his erection was exactly on target and she wanted nothing more than to shift her hips forward, feel him slide inside of her. Shane didn't move, but instead watched her face, waited for her okay, which meant he had more willpower than her.

"I...uh...protection?"

He rolled his eyes, as if astonished he'd forgotten such a thing, then reached past her to the shelf above the bunk and pulled down a small box. In it were Band-Aids, butterfly sutures and a packet of condoms. "Everything a bronc rider needs," she murmured.

"Amen." He opened the package and almost before he was done taking care of business, Ella wrapped her legs back around him, pulling him to where she wanted him. Dead center between her thighs. He met her gaze and smiled a little as his erection once again pressed against her, a slow sensual smile that curved those wickedly perfect lips and stoked the heat threatening to melt her from the inside out—a smile that clearly said, "I'm going to do things you're going to like."

Yes. Please.

Ella arched her hips, pressing herself that much closer, shifting as he began to push into her, his hard length filling her to capacity as he slid all the way home. Her eyes drifted shut at the heady sensation of having him so deeply inside of her.

"Look at me."

She opened her eyes. Found his face close to hers.

"Don't stop," she murmured, bringing a hand up his cheek.

A faint twitch of his lips before he pulled back then sank into her again. "Wasn't going to."

Her hand left his cheek and gripped his shoulder as sensual pleasure rocked her.

"Do that again."

Shane complied, pulling out, then smoothly driving home. Again. And again.

It took Ella a few moments to realize that the low breathy cries she heard reverberating through the trailer were coming from her as she clung to Shane, answering his thrusts. She bit her lip, squeezed her eyes shut, concentrated on the perfect way their bodies fit together, then concentrated even harder on not coming too soon. She wanted this to last…forever maybe.

No. Not forever. But for longer than it was going to.

They fit together so well.

She gave a gasp as the first tremor hit her, pressing her face to Shane's muscular shoulder, once again tasting dust and sweat as her body shuddered against his in rolling waves of pleasure. Before the last wave passed, he gave a series of quick short thrusts and then buried himself to the hilt, every muscle in his body going taut. Ella raised her head in time to see his mouth open in a silent cry of pleasure. The best O face she'd ever seen.

She let her head fall forward onto his damp shoulder, exhaling as he ran a soothing hand over her equally damp back. They stayed that way for a long moment, supporting one another as they recovered, then he maneuvered his way up into the bunk, pulling her with him until they were lying side by side, their bodies pressed together.

"Are you okay?" he finally asked.

Ella laughed, the throaty sound perfectly expressing her current state of mind—sensual and satisfied. "I think you're good for me, Shane Marvell."

He looped his arm a little more tightly around her. "How so?"

She simply smiled, not wanting to ruin the moment with analysis. She was merely expressing the foremost thought in her mind.

He touched his forehead to hers in a tender gesture. "Not too much too soon?"

"In one of my normal relationships, yes." It was the first

time she'd ever done anything like this. "But I feel good. Really good."

He hesitated long enough before responding to cause her to wonder if he felt differently, and if she was the first woman he'd made love too since being dumped in December. That probably *would* make her a rebound girl.

"No regrets?"

"Not one. I'm trying to live my life differently. Explore new options."

"Are you now?"

"Mmm hmm."

"And what are your conclusions at this point?"

"More data is needed."

He laughed and then nipped her lower lip. "We can arrange that. All I'm asking is that you be upfront with me, Ella."

"And you with me?"

"Of course."

She brought her hand up to smooth his hair away from his face, her insides starting to tingle as his eyes met hers.

She'd just found her summer adventure.

"WHERE HAVE YOU been?" Avery yawned as she came into the kitchen wearing her oversized MSU Bobcats T-shirt a few seconds after Ella had let herself into the farmhouse kitchen. A reasonable question, since it was well after 1:00

a.m. and Ella never stayed out late. She'd planned on slipping in quietly without waking either Avery or Jenna and coming up with a story by breakfast, but now…well, where did she begin?

"Are you all right?" Avery asked, her expression one of growing concern.

"Of course. Why?" Ella's attempt at nonchalance felt sadly flat. She was a horrible liar.

"You look shook."

Because she was. As soon as she parted company with Shane, the "what the hell were you thinking?" thoughts started crowding into her brain. But just as rapidly, her I-wouldn't-have-missed-that-for-anything side shot them down. The mental battle was exhausting—and apparently it showed.

"Ella?" Avery's voice took on a worried note.

"I just did something crazy."

"You?"

"Yeah. Me."

"Did it involve a guy?" The question was half teasing, but Ella must have looked shifty, because a look of dawning understanding transformed Avery's face. Her mouth formed a perfect O. "Really?"

Ella nodded.

"Shane?"

She nodded again.

"Wow." The word was drawn out on a long breath. "I

guess we'll have to change your nickname."

Ella gave her friend a warning look. She'd been known as Wait-Until-the-Tenth-Date Ella since her freshman year, and while she'd never before had a problem with that reputation, because it was true, she didn't need it brought to her attention now.

"No harm intended," Avery said. She let out a sigh and plopped into a tubular aluminum kitchen chair. "I don't know whether to be worried or to congratulate you."

Ella went to the fridge and pulled out a beer, which she felt like opening with her teeth. Instead she used the magnetic opener attached to the door. After the cap clattered onto the counter, she took one very long swig. And she didn't immediately pick the cap up, which was as out of character as soothing her jangled nerves with alcohol was.

"Do you regret it?" Avery asked cautiously.

Ella wiped her mouth. "No. That's why *I'm* worried. I don't regret it one bit, but it seems like I should. Right? I mean...this is not me."

"Maybe it's the hidden you."

"Apparently so. I wanted to live differently this summer. Take a few risks. I never dreamed—"

"Tell me you used a condom."

"Of course we used a condom," she said shortly. Two of them as a matter of fact. And not at the same time. "It wasn't like I got swept away in a moment of passion. Well, I did, but that came later. After the condom."

Avery's eyes widened at Ella's candid admission, then she grinned appreciatively.

"TMI?" Ella asked.

"I'll let you know when you've crossed the line. Sheesh. Ella." Avery spread her palms in a who-would-have-thunk-it gesture. "I'm not sure what to say. Way to go?"

Ella laughed and took a seat on the chair opposite her friend. "I wanted him and I went for it, instead of waiting for him to come to me."

"What now?"

Ella bit her lip briefly. "I may never see him again, or he may go on to be my summer adventure."

"Just the summer?"

The thought gave her pause. For once in her life she didn't want to look too far into the future.

"I'm trying to be realistic, but nothing is like it used to be, so I don't know."

"I think it's a good thing that you didn't get that research position. I think that was the kick in the butt you needed."

"Agreed," Ella said as she took another drink of beer, then pushed it aside. Enough nerve soothing. Avery made a good point. Ella wasn't a wuss when push came to shove, but she also hadn't been hanging herself out there, risking failure, humiliation, or ever minor embarrassment—the things she understood and empathized with when they happened to other people, but was afraid to deal with herself.

She shifted in her chair, felt the aftermath of a couple of

hours of lovemaking. She was sore, but in a good way. "There's something about this guy, Ave. If I never hook up with him again, I'll regret it, but I'll be okay. But the fact that I did…" her lips curved into a slow, satisfied smile "…kind of changed my outlook on life." Even more than losing the assistantship, and in a much more pleasant way.

Avery didn't smile back. Instead her fair brows came together in a slight frown, telling Ella that while her friend was happy for her, she also had concerns. "I'm glad. Just…be careful, okay?"

As she thought. No one seemed to have much faith in her abilities to step out of her comfort zone and return unscathed.

Ella begged to differ. There had to be a fine line between careful and too careful, and she was going to find it and walk it.

~

SHANE ROLLED OVER in his bunk and automatically reached for Ella, only to find her side of the bed empty and cold. He'd understood her decision to leave the night before, but wished she'd stayed. Wished the bed didn't feel so damned empty without her. He was kind of stunned at how empty it felt.

Because it's been months and months since you've had anyone there.

He flopped over on his back and stared up at the ceiling, only a few feet above him. Things had felt different when he'd woken up in his empty bed after Darcy exited his life. In addition to the empty space, there was anger, self-blame, regret crowding in on him, telling him things could have been different had he just opened his eyes and seen life the way she did.

He and Ella hadn't gotten to the point where they needed to see life the same way, and they probably never would. He'd win his money, figure out what kind of training he needed to earn some kind of living, see about obtaining financing to buy a small home of his own. Ella'd go back to academia, pursue her studies. But in the meantime, like she'd said, it felt as if they were good for one another. He was about to embark on a summer romance. Go figure.

Shane pushed himself up on his good elbow, his shoulder protesting even that slight movement, which didn't bode well for that day's ride. But he wasn't the only guy hurting. The trick was to be better at muscling through than everyone he was competing against.

He slid to the edge of the bunk and eased down, his face contorting with pain. His knee felt like it was the size of a balloon—mainly because his knee *was* the size of a balloon.

Shit.

He braced his hands on his thighs and took a couple of deep, head-clearing breaths. *Walk it off.*

He took a couple painful steps toward the bathroom. The swelling was always at its worst in the morning and he had given his knees a workout the night before—until Ella had taken over and flipped him onto his back. He did love a woman who took charge. If Ella was the shrinking violet of her family, then he was kind of afraid to meet the rest of them.

They'd made no plans to meet, both apparently assuming they'd run into each other when it happened. She had bull riders to talk to and he had to take a drive to a nearby town to look at a tractor for Zach. He would have liked to have her along, but something told him that it wouldn't take much to spook her. He wanted to continue their easy no-pressure relationship, so he was by himself two hours later when he left Dillon to drive south to Dell.

He'd taped his knee and wore his brace to give it enough support to operate the clutch. It worked, even if he did kind of feel like tearing up when he shifted gears. It was almost enough to make him want to invest in an automatic. Almost. He actually had better things to spend his money on. Like his future.

Which made winning the B.B. Gilmore bonus all the more imperative. He didn't know how long his body was going to cooperate and he needed to rack up the points while he could.

IT WAS HARD to focus on bull riders when all she could think about was bronc riders. Or rather *a* bronc rider. Ella muscled through her late-afternoon interviews, reviewed her notes while sitting in her truck, added a few personal observations while they were fresh in her head.

And she looked for Shane's truck.

His trailer was right where it'd been when she'd left the night before, but the gooseneck was sitting on a sturdy wooden block. No truck to be seen.

Focus, girl.

Kind of hard to when flashes of memory kept sending sensual tremors through her body. To be honest, her experiences with lovemaking in the past had involved a healthy dose of awkwardness in the beginning, as she and her partner figured out the good, the bad, and the don't-go-there. She'd never had an experience like the one she'd shared with Shane, where they seemed to automatically know what would please the other. Maybe it was her new go-for-it attitude, or maybe it was just that his body meshed so well with her own. And that he had a very talented tongue and wasn't afraid to use it.

Whatever, the experience had been blissfully satisfying.

One she hoped to repeat.

The throb of a diesel brought her head up as Shane's truck approached along the narrow grassy path between trailers and horses and her heartbeat stuttered. Her first instinct was deeply engrained—stay where she was. That was the safe response. Her second was to man up and get a read on the situation. If he wasn't going to be her summer adventure, if she'd had a glorious one-night stand, she wanted to know about it now.

Ella got out of her truck and headed for where Shane was positioning himself to hook up the trailer. He started to get out, then saw her and closed the door again. Without a word, Ella went to the rear of his truck and dropped the tailgate. Shane backed up under the gooseneck until Ella waved her hand, bringing him to a stop before she started cranking the trailer down onto the ball in the bed of the truck. It slid easily into place, so she finished cranking while Shane got out of the rig and limped closer.

"I'll get the latch," she said, climbing over the side of the truck and dropping the pin through the latch before reaching for the safety chains.

"Wish you'd been here this morning."

Ella stilled at his quiet words, then latched the safety chains. He wasn't only talking about help with the trailer. Liquid heat started to pool within her midsection. "Me, too."

She stood and swung a leg over the side of the truck. Shane held out his hand as she perched her butt on the edge and then jumped to the ground, landing lightly beside him. His fingers closed around hers, quelling any thoughts she'd had about their night being a one-time thing.

"Were you sightseeing?" she asked.

"My brother, Zach, wanted me to see about a tractor." He shook his head. "It looked good on paper, but too many issues. Cody might like it as a project, but we're not paying that kind of money for a project."

Ella dusted off her hands, needing to do something with them to keep from putting them on Shane. "You don't have much time to get ready."

"I have enough. Will I see you after the rodeo?"

The warmth in her belly intensified. "Yes."

He gave her a crooked half-smile. "Good." He took a stiff step forward, toward the trailer and Ella frowned. He had his brace on over his pants, but she suspected his knee was also taped.

"A little trouble with the clutch?"

"I managed."

She gave a nod. It wasn't her place to judge what he did or did not do. He touched her then. Reached out and laid his palm on her cheek. "I'm good to buck tonight."

He'd read her thoughts.

"Of course." Because that was what bronc riders did. They cowboyed up until they broke down to the point that they couldn't. She suspected that Shane was close to that point. It seemed crazy to continue to compete when injury intensified the chances of being hurt even worse, but Ella kept her mouth firmly shut. She might have shared his bed, but they were not at the point where she could offer her take on a touchy subject.

"I'll see you afterward." His hand fell away. Ella gave him a quick smile and turned toward her truck. He needed time to stretch and tape his shoulder and get into his head.

He didn't need her distracting him.

And she didn't need to be worried about him. He was doing what he wanted to do, but she couldn't help wonder, as she did with her siblings, how the payoff was worth the risk.

She pulled her hat a little lower over her eyes as she walked past her truck and headed in the direction of Avery and Jenna's trailer. She might be loosening up, taking minor risks, but for the life of her, she did not get why some people did the things they did. She didn't know whether to be disappointed in herself or resigned to the fact that she was who she was.

SHANE'S RIDE WAS perfect—right up until the seven-second mark, which was when Twister did just that, throwing Shane off over his hand a split second before the buzzer. He managed to crack his elbow open, start to release the glove, but it was too little, too late. He sailed off the wrong side of the horse, and his shoulder was nearly wrenched out of the socket when his gloved hand remained in the rigging. He flopped once on the side of the horse before getting hold of the glove and pulling it free of the rigging. His knee would have buckled when he went down if it hadn't been for the brace.

Pain nearly split him in two, but he forced himself up out of the dirt and headed toward the gate. It wasn't until it swung open that he realized he was hunched inward, holding his shoulder with his gloved hand.

Ella was there, just outside the gate. "I'll get your rigging," she said.

He managed a nod and headed toward his trailer, which seemed a long, long ways from where he was.

"Shane!"

He looked over his shoulder at Tyson. One of the sports medicine guys was standing next to him, but Shane shook his head. He knew what the problem was, and knew that there wasn't a hell of a lot they could do after the fact.

He reached his trailer and had to try twice to get his leg up onto the step. On the second attempt someone put a firm hand on his back. Ella. He managed the step and then sank down on the bunk.

She set his rigging in the corner, then stood a few feet away from him, as if debating her next move. And Shane was torn between telling her he'd manage on his own, or to accept the help she was silently offering.

He went with help. Ella read his answer in his face and he leaned forward so that she could help him ease out of his vest. He bit his lip to keep from wincing as he worked his arm free.

"How bad?"

"Not dislocated, but it stings."

She gave a short laugh, but there was no humor in it. He stood and undid the buckle of his chaps, letting them fall to the floor. A puff of arena dust erupted into the air. Ella picked up the dusty chaps and tossed them on top of the rigging.

"Sit down and I'll get your boots."

After the boots came his shirt, his jeans. Her touch was gentle but sure, and he wished he was in a condition to appreciate the way her hands felt on his skin, but his shoulder was shouting too loudly. After his jeans landed on top of the chaps, he sat and tilted his head back as Ella expertly peeled the brace off his knee. Then she sat back on her heels, meeting his gaze. "What about the tape?"

The truth was, he didn't want anything touching his throbbing shoulder. "Leave it for now."

"Painkillers?"

He swallowed dryly. "Next to the sink."

She got to her feet, found the bottles of generic ibuprofen and acetaminophen, shook a few pills out of each, then handed them to him along with the bottle of water that had been sitting beside the pill containers.

"That enough?"

"It'll do." But no. Nothing short of Percocet was going to be enough at this point.

"I need to take care of a few details."

Details? Fine. He just wanted to crawl into the bunk and let the drugs take what little effect they would have. And he wanted Ella there, too. Not touching him, but there. He didn't want to think about what that meant.

By the time she got back in the trailer, Shane was dressed in a T-shirt and sweats. She didn't need to know that he'd broken into a sweat putting them on.

"Details taken care of?"

"Yeah. Now the only question is, do you want to leave tonight or tomorrow morning?" He frowned at her, not fully understanding her meaning. She cocked a hip and set her hand on it. "I'm driving you back to Marietta. All I need to know is when do you want to leave?"

"How are you getting back to your truck?"

"Avery has an appointment in Bozeman tomorrow. She'll pick me up."

Shane's instincts said that he needed to man up. Drive the damned truck himself.

His knee said, "Fuck that."

Shane went with the knee and managed a smile. "Looks like I have a driver."

Chapter Nine

"I'D LIKE TO sleep in the trailer."

Shane hadn't argued with Ella about driving him to the ranch. Normally he wasn't prone to accepting help, but it made sense in this circumstance. He'd have had a difficult time making the drive, and he wanted to spend time with Ella. Not that he'd been much company on the drive home, having fallen asleep before they hit the freeway at Rocker. He'd woken up outside of Marietta, and given her directions. A little less than an hour later, they'd driven under the lightning-struck log arch that marked the entrance to the ranch.

"I won't fight you on it," Shane said, reaching for his door handle. "I'll just tell my brother that we're here." It was after midnight. The kitchen lights were off, but a faint glow illuminated the curtained window of Zach's office.

"And you should probably sleep in your bed in the house instead of trying to climb into the bunk."

It appeared that Ella didn't want to shout out to the world that she was sleeping with him and he would respect that.

"Probably," he agreed.

She reached out to slide her hand down his pain-free arm. "I don't want you hurting yourself and if you stay with me," she said in a way that made his groin stir despite drugs and rampant pain, "there's a better than average chance that you will."

He took hold of her hand, laced his fingers with hers. "That kind of talk isn't going to get me into a separate bed."

She tilted her chin up to meet his lips in the briefest of kisses. "Humor me tonight."

"Will do. But you may as well come inside and use the facilities. Shower if you want to. Then you can go to bed in the trailer."

And he'd ease himself down into his lonely bed. "What time do you need to be in Bozeman tomorrow?"

"Not until the afternoon." Ella tucked her hair behind her ear as they walked across the gravel drive to the house.

"Maybe you could stay at the ranch a day or two." The invitation surprised him almost as much as it surprised her.

Ella's eyes widened ever so slightly. "Yeah?" she asked softly.

"Stay on the ranch, go with me to the Red Rock rodeo." Which he was doing instead of White Sulphur Springs so that his knee had an extra couple of days. "You can hook up with Avery there."

Ella hesitated just a little too long, and a stab of disappointment shot through him. He gave a casual shrug with his uninjured shoulder, then reached for the screen door handle.

"Or not. I only thought that it might be a way for us to enjoy what's left of summer."

Before the rodeo season ended and she headed back to Nevada and her studies.

Ella smiled a little. "It makes sense. I mean…there's not much summer left, is there?"

"We should take the opportunities we have. If you want to, that is. No pressure."

Her expression didn't shift as she said, "That's probably why I'm going to say yes."

Shane grinned as he pulled open the door and stood back to allow her to precede him into the dark kitchen. A chair moved back in Zach's office and Shane called, "Don't come out if you're not decent." He glanced down at Ella. "My brother tends to do his accounts in his boxers on hot nights." And this was a hot night.

Zach appeared in the doorway next to the kitchen, blinking first at Shane, then Ella.

"Ella drove me home. She's sleeping in the trailer."

"Why?"

"Because she wants to."

"Cody's not due back until morning. She can have his room."

"Thanks," Ella said. "But I'll just use the bathroom and go back to the trailer."

"Suit yourself." Zach cocked a dark eyebrow. "And good to meet you." He ran his gaze over Shane as if looking for open wounds or another reason he might have to be driven home.

"Went off over my hand. Wrenched the shoulder. Hurts like hell."

Zach gave a silent nod, then jerked his head toward his computer. "I'll just shut down and call it a night."

He disappeared back into the office and Shane pointed out the bathroom door to Ella. "I'll be one door down if you need anything."

"I won't." She sounded sure of it. "But thanks, Shane. I'll see you in the morning."

"LET ME GET this straight." Ella leveled a hard look across the table at Shane. "You're too injured to drive, but you're going to mend fence?"

Shane spun his empty coffee cup in a slow circle. "Part of the deal I made with my brothers. Rodeo wouldn't get in the way of my ranch duties. As it is, they work around my schedule."

Ella gave a considering nod. "Fine. I'll come with you."

"For the record, that isn't why I asked you to stay."

"No kidding?" she asked on a husky note. She had no difficulty discerning the reason he'd wanted her to stay. It was the same reason she'd said yes—to continue their excellent adventure. Or as he had put it, to take advantage of what was left of the summer. The only thing was his brothers. If she was the first woman he'd brought home since being dumped, then they were going to wonder. And while she told herself it didn't matter what they thought, for some reason it did, which was why she didn't want to share Shane's bed. Not openly anyway. She wanted to be there under the guise of being a friend—they were friends after all—which would leave Shane with a lot fewer questions to answer or dodge once she was gone.

Despite his shoulder, Shane had been up and cooking when she'd come into the house that morning to use the bathroom and shower. By the time she'd gotten out, breakfast was on the table along with a handful of daisies stuck in a mason jar. She'd smiled at the whimsy, then loaded her plate with scrambled eggs and potatoes. Shane's potatoes were almost as good as her father's and she'd done them justice.

"I'll help with the fence," Ella said. "Where's your brother?"

"Zach is already out feeding, and Cody should be back at any time now. We have a couple of guys working for us, but they're both off right now and Zach is taking up the slack."

"Does he sleep?"

Shane let out a short breath as he pushed himself to his feet. "He's been running this ranch since he was fifteen and I don't think he's slept more than six hours a night since he took over."

"Fifteen?"

"Our dad got killed in an accident. My mom had a hard time coping. Zach took over."

"Wow."

"Yeah. He's focused on the ranch for so long, I don't know if he's capable of focusing on anything else."

"No wife or girlfriend?"

"No wife. Girlfriends get tired of coming in second to the ranch."

She propped her elbows on the table. "How about you? Are you deeply tied to the ranch?"

"I love working here, being part of the legacy."

But she sensed he was holding something back. "Do you plan to stay here?"

"Yes." Again, there was something in his tone that told Ella not to push the matter. Instead she got up and filled her coffee cup. She held up the pot, Shane nodded, and she filled his cup, too.

"I talked to Avery. Jenna will drive my truck to Red Rock, so I'll have wheels when I get there."

When she looked back, he was studying her with an odd expression.

"What?" She felt color start to rise in her face. He was so damned good-looking, it was all she could do not to cross the room and straddle his lap, push her fingers into his hair and take advantage of that perfect mouth.

"I appreciate you driving me home."

She gave a not-a-problem shrug, studying him almost as intently as he was studying her before saying, "I appreciate the opportunity to see your ranch."

"It feels like things are moving fast."

Okay. Honesty. She was good with that.

"Are you willing to hang on and see where the ride takes us?"

His gorgeous mouth curved ever so slightly as a smile lit his eyes. "I like the way you put that."

"It's the way I see it."

"Do you need a place to work while you're here? To, you know, put together your notes or whatever?"

She was touched he would think of such a thing. "I might let things percolate for a while in my brain." She smiled slowly. "You know, while I mend fence."

"It's a never-ending job."

"I know. I've been fencing since I was old enough to hold pliers."

"Then I made a wise decision asking you to stay."

She gave him a smile that bordered on wicked. She wasn't thinking about fencing. "So it seems."

He held out a hand. "Come here."

It was a request, not a demand, so Ella went, taking her time as she crossed the room. As she'd told Avery, there was something about this guy that made her feel confident. Like she could do anything if she put her mind to it. Maybe this was what it felt like when one stopped hiding behind textbooks and worrying about the trouble one could get into if they didn't measure every move in life.

No. Obviously, this *was* what it felt like.

Heady stuff, and it got headier when Shane took her hand and pulled her a few steps closer. "If you ever get to the point where you regret anything about our wild ride, you tell me."

"Maybe we need a safe word."

He grinned. "Name it."

She leaned down, bringing her face close to his before raising her eyebrows and saying, "How about I'll just take my chances?" Her voice sounded like a sensual purr. And she didn't feel one bit self-conscious about it. His breath was warm against her face, his mouth so tantalizingly close. How could she pull back without touching those perfect lips?

Ella kissed him, lightly teasing his lips, breathing in his scent as she drew back, loving how it made her feel like eating him alive. She saw the unmistakable flash of desire in his eyes, so she kissed him again, first teasing his tongue, then paying the price as he took control of the kiss, maneuvering her onto his lap as he took his time exploring her lips, her mouth, the sensitive area near her temple. She had some vague thoughts about not wanting to hurt the injured parts of his body, but the erection pressing into her leg made her believe that he wasn't particularly concerned about pain and injury at the moment.

The phone buzzed in her shirt pocket, startling her. Ella leaned back to pull it out of the tight pocket, fumbled, and sent it flying. The phone clattered onto the floor and slid under the table, but not before she saw Finley's name on the screen.

"My sister." She slid off his lap. "I should take this. Someone is probably in the hospital." She was only half kidding. Calls from home always terrified her. She'd barely hit redial when the sound of an engine approaching had both she and Shane craning their necks to look out the kitchen window. A classic GMC truck pulled to a stop next to Shane's truck and trailer.

"I think our siblings are in cahoots," Shane muttered. "That's my brother, Cody."

"I'm looking forward to meeting him—" She turned away as her sister picked up. "Finley. What's up?" She almost said, "What now?"

"Have you been out of the cell service area?"

"Maybe on and off, but for the most part, no. Why?"

"Because I got a call on the ranch line from a John Bruch."

"Dr. Bruch?" Ella held the phone a little tighter. "He should have my cell number."

"Well the one he's using isn't working. I wanted to make certain you know who the guy was before I gave out your contact information. He asked if I could have you call him."

"Okay. I might." She met Shane's gaze briefly.

"Who is he?" Finley asked.

"The guy who didn't hire me. If he calls back, give him my cell number."

A tall dark-haired version of Shane walked into the kitchen and did a double take when he saw Ella standing near the fridge, cell phone at her ear. She smiled at him, then turned her attention back to the call. "Give me a sec, Finley."

"Use Zach's office," Shane said.

"Thanks. Shouldn't be long." She smiled at Shane's brother again, and headed down the hall. "Okay, Finn, when did he call…?"

CODY LOOKED AT Shane as Ella left, his expression holding elements of both surprise and admiration. "You brought home a guest?"

"She drove me home because I couldn't. Not safely, anyway."

"She's your chauffer."

Shane smiled benignly. "Yes. And she'll be going to Red Rock with me where she'll hook up with her truck."

"Red Rock is not for three days."

"Good thing. I need the healing time."

"Little brother…" Cody shook his head in a weary way.

There was a wealth of meaning in the gesture and Shane opened his mouth to defend himself, a knee-jerk reaction that came from being the youngest and constantly monitored by two nosy older brothers, but Cody put up a hand, stopping him.

"I know why you're riding injured. I get it. I really do. But are you sure you're going to survive this season? I've never seen you so beat up."

"I'm getting old." There were guys on the circuit older than him who were faring better injury-wise, but not points-wise. At this juncture, he'd take the points. "You know how it goes. You adjust for one injury and it causes another because you aren't using your body in the way you trained."

"If you say so."

"I can't exactly quit. What will I have?"

"You might want to think about what you'll have—or not have—if you don't quit."

"I'll be fine," Shane said. He meant it. He just needed to hang on for three more rodeos and the finals. He was far enough ahead that if he muffed one, he could still win overall. It was a good place to be. Grit and determination had gotten him there, and grit and determination would see him through.

The door to the office opened and Ella came back into the kitchen a few seconds later. She slipped the phone into her back pocket and crossed the linoleum to hold out a hand to Cody in a businesslike way.

"I would have known you as Shane's brother had we met elsewhere. You look just like him."

"Cody, meet Ella. Ella, my brother, Cody." Shane absently massaged his injured shoulder as he made the introductions. "Ella is doing research into risk behaviors in rodeo athletes."

Cody's eyebrows lifted. "Research?"

"Not an official study yet. I'm collecting data to write a grant proposal to fund the research and my master's degree."

Cody looked impressed, as Shane had known he would. Cody did love a woman with smarts. Shane was beginning to feel the same way. He shoved the thought aside and forged on.

"Ella and I are going to mend fence today. Want to come?"

"If I do, who will fix the baler so that we can mow the hay in dire need of cutting?"

"Good point." Cody turned back to Ella. "First time fixing fence?"

A sputtering laugh left her lips, then she quickly pressed her fingers to her mouth. "Sorry. I…no. Not my first time."

Color crept up Cody's neck from his collar as he appeared to realize how condescending he'd sounded. "Sorry I assumed that…hell, I don't know what I assumed." He sent Shane an accusing look, then turned to Ella. "I didn't expect a person researching risk behaviors in rodeo athletes to have fencing skills. My mistake."

"I grew up on a ranch in Nevada," Ella explained. "But the ranch can't support all of us, so I'm chasing a different career."

"And I made a snap judgment." Cody gave her a charming smile. "Nice to meet you, Ella the Nevada ranch kid."

"Likewise, Cody."

Shane pushed his chair back and used the table to maneuver himself to his feet. "We should get to work." He wanted to put a little distance between his brother and the woman he'd brought to the ranch, which kind of floored him, but there was no denying his reaction to Cody's gentle flirtation.

Mine.

It was enough to give a guy pause.

Chapter Ten

ELLA HAD NO idea why Dr. Bruch wanted to get in contact with her, and the beauty part was that she didn't care all that much. Not now, anyway. She had three days on a beautiful ranch with a guy she liked, and she wasn't going to wallow in anxiety.

Her current attitude should have made her stomach squeeze itself into a tight ball as she worried about *why* she had that attitude, and what it might mean to her future, but it didn't. Instead she felt a tingle of anticipation as she helped Shane load tools into the UTV—an all-terrain vehicle that looked similar to a dune buggy with a utility bed in back.

Hello, New Ella. How long will you be with us?

Until you get into deep trouble and I have to rescue you, Old Ella muttered back.

"And that should do it," Shane said as he put a cooler in the back of the UTV.

There were sandwiches, water and beer in the cooler. It wasn't so much of a work day as a reconnaissance day. They might repair easy spots, but Shane was doing a general survey in preparation for winter, when the change of temperatures and the weight of the snow made the fences sag. Best to have them as tight as possible before the weather arrived.

Ella settled into her seat beside Shane and they headed toward a gate leading to a broad pasture, which she opened so that Shane could drive through. The lot of the passenger: opening gates. She would have opened them even if she'd been driving. Shane was having a hard time getting around and it kind of killed her to think of him climbing aboard a bronc in a matter of days to risk hurting himself all over again. But he was doing what he had to do, and she was in a perfect situation to explore his thought processes, his reasoning, his goals.

Instead she focused on the beauty of their surroundings, because she'd be facing the reality of his chosen profession soon enough. The ranch was nestled close to the mountains, and after they crossed the pasture, they drove into a belt of trees, then emerged again close to a small river that wound its way through another meadow.

If the Marvells sold this ranch, they would be rolling in money. And have to come up with another way to make a living.

"How long has this ranch been in your family?"

"Since the turn of the century. My great-great-grandfather and his brothers founded it. Then there was a rift between them after World War I and one of the brothers went north to the Flathead Lake area to found our sister ranch."

"A sister ranch? Interesting."

"Our horse trainer is engaged to one of my cousins, so he's helping on the Marvell North, which is leaving us a little shorthanded down here."

"Will he stay after they get married?"

Shane shot her a look. "I'm guessing not, so we'll be looking for a guy to take over that job. And our other regular employee is looking at college next year, so…yeah. Maybe a good thing I'm retiring after this season."

"How can the three of you keep up with this place?" As near as she could tell, it was a good-size spread.

"We have a couple summer day hands to help with the irrigating and general upkeep. Usually one of them would be traveling with me and would finish up whatever we started this week while I'm on the road, but I thought the UTV would be kind of crowded with three of us."

Ella laughed. She was glad it was just the two of them.

"WHAT'S HAPPENING WITH your research?" Shane crumpled a sandwich wrapper and tossed it into the empty cooler.

Ella gave him a curious look. They'd stopped for lunch in a grassy meadow, ate sandwiches and shared a beer. Had he been thinking about her research the entire time she'd been reveling in *not* thinking about it?

"How close are you to writing your proposal?" he specified.

"It's due October thirtieth, with possible funding in January if I get it."

"Not exactly an answer to the question."

She frowned as she twisted a weed between her fingers. "I'm procrastinating."

"And that's when you ask yourself why."

"Burnout?" The words slipped off her tongue so automatically that she knew they were true. She was burned out. Tired of pushing herself. Tired of worry. She rolled over onto her stomach and propped herself up on her elbows. "Like I told Cody, the ranch can't support us all. I have to have a career. I was going to teach, because it's a profession where I could live close to home, but you know what? I found out I was a lot more relaxed away from home. That made me want to do something else, like study sports psychology." She made a face. "Does that make me a bad sister and daughter?"

Shane tapped her nose with a long piece of grass. "That probably makes you the person who took responsibility for everyone else."

"How do you know that?"

"Because Cody does the same thing. I recognize the signs."

"Huh." She rolled back over onto her back, staring up into the cerulean blue sky. A bald eagle flew overhead and she smiled. In Nevada, golden eagles were common, bald eagles rare. Here bald eagles were almost like sparrows.

"You said you were breaking free, trying to be like the rest of your family."

"Yeah? So?"

"That's probably a sign of burnout, too."

"Possibly," she agreed, "although I didn't get the assistantship that would have paid for graduate school because I wasn't like the rest of my family, which might be another motivator. That was when I decided to research risk behaviors on my own."

"And to show him? Meaning the guy who didn't hire you?"

Ella smiled a little. "Maybe. That's the Etxeberri coming out. We're all highly competitive."

Shane smiled back then reached out to take hold of her shoulders and pull her on top of him as he rolled onto his back. "What would *that* be like?"

She kissed his chin, teasing the short bristles there with her lips, loving the feel of her body weighing him down. "Yes. Indeed. If only there was someone around that I could compete with."

He pushed his fingers through her hair. "In what arena?"

"Well, you're a wreck, no offense intended, so it won't be a foot race."

"You want to compete with me?"

She considered for a moment. "No. I want to have my

way with you."

He grinned wickedly. "Here? For the eagles and woodland creatures to see?"

"If you don't think any day hands will wander by, that is exactly what I want."

His expression grew serious. "I can guarantee you that we are far from irrigated fields. No day hands."

"In that case…" She held his gaze as she slid down his body until her hands were at his belt buckle.

"Do it. I dare you."

Slowly she undid the buckle and then she commenced showing Shane Marvell what happened when one issued a dare to an Etch.

~

ELLA HAD A magic touch. Broken as his body was, she made him feel like a superman when they made love. And being with her made him perform like a superman, too, if he did say so himself.

It's the novelty of being with someone new. All fledgling relationships are like this.

The justification didn't ring true. There was something about being with Ella that made him want to do his best. Be his best.

But the sad truth was that he wasn't the best. Yet. He was a broken-down rodeo rider who had a long way to go before he had something decent to offer a woman.

He was getting ahead of himself, but he had to be realistic, not let things get out of hand. By mutual agreement, this was supposed to be a fun summer adventure. Meaningful, yet not too serious. The kind of relationship where they would have fond memories of what they were able to give one another in the short term. He was going to do his best to remember that.

It seemed prophetic, given his thoughts, that Shane spotted Cal Llewelyn's truck parked in front of the main house when he and Ella left the barn after parking the UTV.

He hoped Darcy wasn't there. Not because of the awkwardness—and there would be some—but because Ella would key in to the awkwardness. She was sharp that way, and he didn't want his past intruding on his summer any more than it already was. He thought about asking her if she'd like to see the horses, but as luck would have it, Zach and Cal came out of the house before he could say anything. Cal saw him, and his neck went red.

Great.

"Hey, Cal," he said as casually as he could manage. He sensed Ella giving him a look, but focused on the guy who was now engaged to Darcy. He did his best not to limp too much as he crossed the final bit of gravel to where the truck was parked.

"Shane." Cal descended the steps. "I see you're burning up the circuit this year."

"Well, it is my last season, so I thought I'd make it memorable." Ella stopped next to him, close enough that her shoulder bumped his upper arm in a companionable way. He glanced down and she gave him a pleasant half-smile. Two people comfortable being close to one another. He answered her smile with a quick twitch of his lips.

"Cal, this is Ella Etxeberri. She's researching risk behavior in rodeo athletes. I'm showing her the ranch."

Ella moved her braid over her shoulder as she stepped forward to offer her hand to Cal, who looked slightly bemused, yet also relieved, as if he'd just been absolved of a measure of guilt.

"Nice to meet you, Ella. I'm Cal. I help with the business end of things for various ranches."

"Nice to meet you," she echoed before moving back to Shane's side. He had to admit that having Ella with him while coming face-to-face with Cal for the first time since Darcy agreed to marry the guy made the encounter more palatable—for both him and Cal.

"Well, my work is done here," Cal said briskly. He glanced at Zach. "See you at the rodeo board meeting?"

"No doubt," Zach said. The Copper Mountain Rodeo was coming up fast and there were last-minute details to work out.

"Final tweaks to the security teams and stuff like that," Cal explained to Shane. "Looking forward to watching your ride."

Shane smiled and touched his ball cap, and then, just because, he looped a casual arm around Ella's shoulders.

"You guys hungry?" Zach asked after Cal drove away. He didn't seem surprised at Shane and Ella's casual embrace. "I have a stew on."

"He cooks, too?" Ella murmured after Zach turned and headed back into the house. Shane dropped his arm.

"Zach's a catch," he said with a half-smile. "If you don't mind—"

"Being second to the ranch." She grinned at him as they walked to the door. "I'm not in the market for a catch."

"Yeah? What are you in the market for?"

She waggled her eyebrows and he laughed, but there was a softness in her expression that kind of did something to him, made him feel all tender and mushy inside. He opened the screen door and held it as she ducked under his arm. He wasn't ready to feel that way.

So he wouldn't.

Fat chance, buddy. You're already sliding down the slippery slope.

It didn't seem possible, but the fact that he had to struggle not to reach out and set his hand on the small of her back as they walked into the kitchen told him, yeah. He might be farther gone than he'd thought.

ELLA'S SECOND DAY on the ranch promised to be as beautiful as the first. She rolled over the bunk over the gooseneck of Shane's fancy horse trailer and stretched, enjoying the slant of sunlight shining in through the window at the end of the bunk. The bed smelled like Shane and every time she breathed into his pillow, she smiled. It'd be nice if he was there with her, but they'd get their time together today. She wasn't ready to share a bed with him in his brother's house.

She hadn't called Dr. Bruch yet. Didn't know if she was going to. She also didn't know if it was because she wasn't ready to make any hard and fast decisions about school and assistantships and future study, or if it was because she was insulating herself from reality while she was on the Marvell ranch. She'd be leaving in a matter of days, following the rodeo to Red Rock, meeting up with Avery and Jenna, probably answering a bunch of questions.

A rap on the door brought her head up. She pushed her hair out of her face as Shane cracked the door open.

"Just thought I'd let you know that the shower is free, which it won't be once Cody gets out of bed."

"A shower sounds lovely." She swung her legs out of bed. She couldn't quite sit up straight because of the low ceiling, so she eased down to the floor as Shane came in and closed the door behind him.

"Much as I'd like to, I can't stay."

She didn't think she was imagining the change in Shane since Cal Llewelyn left the ranch, and while it really was none of her business, she wanted to know what the deal was between the two men. And why the aftereffect had lingered on long after Cal had driven away.

But instead of asking the nagging question, she said,

"Then I'll grab a shower and be ready to work in about twenty minutes." She cocked her head. "We are working today, right?"

"I'm a bad host."

"I like to keep busy."

"Oh, I'll keep you busy," Shane said, reaching out to pull her against him. Ella laughed before easing back. "Shower. Coffee. Then you can keep me busy."

"I'll meet you in the shop, next to the barn." He cocked an eyebrow. "Twenty minutes, you say?" He sounded as if he didn't believe it was possible.

"I won't dry my hair. So yeah, twenty minutes."

Shane pulled the old-fashioned watch out of his pocket, noted the time, then slipped it back into place, issuing an unspoken challenge. Ella appreciated a man who had a watch instead of a phone, and she also appreciated a challenge.

"Shall we make it interesting?" Ella asked, assuming it would be a win-win situation for her.

"Sure. Winner names the prize." He stepped out of the horse trailer, closing the door behind him. Ella's lips twitched as she gathered her clothes, pulled on her jeans, then followed him out a few seconds later. Yes. Definitely win-win.

There was no sign of him as she crossed the driveway to the main house, but she heard male voices in the building that she assumed was the shop. Good. Maybe she wasn't going to have to go face-to-face with Zach, who was intimidating in his silence.

She opened the door to an empty kitchen and bypassed the coffeepot to head straight to the bathroom. Once there she started the water in the old-fashioned green-tile bath enclosure, then shucked out of her clothing. The mirror instantly steamed, but she couldn't find a switch for an exhaust fan, so she stepped under the spray and closed her eyes as water soaked her long hair, plastering it to her back. She could have happily stayed under the spray until the hot water tank ran out, but instead Ella washed her hair, scrubbed her body, and turned off the water. The towel she'd used the day before was on the hook where she'd left it, so she toweled off, blotted the water out of her hair, then pulled her underwear and jeans up damp legs. It was so steamy that when she cleared the spot on the mirror with the heel of her hand, it instantly fogged up again. Fine. She slipped on her T-shirt and cracked the door open so that she could see to braid her hair.

"Uh…"

A masculine voice outside made her jump, then she said, "I'm decent. Are you?"

"Close to it."

"Be out in a sec." She picked up the bathmat and hung it over the tub to dry, stuffed her clothing into her bag, then pushed the door the rest of the way open. Cody stood there in his sweats. Yes. That was decent enough.

"Sucks to only have one bathroom," he said.

The house was small, and Ella imagined it had been a challenge to raise three boys in it without the walls coming down. "Lots of people grew up that way," she murmured.

Cody disappeared into the steamy bathroom, and Ella headed for the kitchen. She poured a cup of coffee, checked the time, then pulled her damp hair over her shoulder and began to braid. Loosely. She didn't want to look like Medusa when she undid the braid later. Medusa head would not mesh with the prize she intended to collect from Shane later that day—if the opportunity presented itself.

Time was ticking by, so she abandoned her bag in the kitchen, grabbed the coffee and headed across the driveway to the shop, where Shane was talking to two guys in their late teens, obviously lining them out for the day.

He pulled his watch out when she stepped through the door and his eyebrows lifted appreciatively. "Thirty seconds to spare. You cut it close."

"Your brother slowed me up."

The look on his face would have been comical if the two kids hadn't been there. "We had a brief discussion about one-bathroom houses."

"Ah."

After the kids were lined out and took off on their respective four-wheelers, Shane turned to Ella, who casually sipped her coffee as she leaned back against a tool bench.

"And the prize is...?"

"You tell me about Cal Llewelyn and why he made you

so uncomfortable."

That had not been the prize she'd first thought of, but it was the prize she wanted. What was the deal between the two guys? Not to be dramatic, but the tension had been palpable and when she'd leaned closer to him, he'd echoed the movement, as if drawing strength from her.

Shane let out a breath and ran a hand over the back of his neck as he stared down at the oil-stained concrete floor. When he looked up at her again, she knew that she'd asked for the wrong prize. She should have gone with the obvious—what they were both expecting, regardless of who won—but she hadn't and suddenly the stakes were raised in their easy summer adventure. She was getting personal.

And how telling was it that she could have said, "*Never mind, none of my business,*" but she didn't.

"Cal is engaged to the woman I'd hoped to marry."

Ella's mouth fell open. "I...wow. The one who turned you down?"

That's it, Ella. Twist the knife. She was taking a bad situation and making it worse.

"Yeah." The word dropped heavily. "I asked her in December. She said no, after being together for two years. Eight months later, she's heading to the altar. They'll be married before the end of the year."

Ella set her coffee cup on the bench. "Sorry," she murmured.

"For?" The word was lightly spoken, but Shane had, for

all intents and purposes, shut down. When she'd named her prize, she'd struck a nerve. A big one.

"Not going for the prize that would have made us both happy."

Shane rubbed his neck again, then dropped his hand loosely back to his side. "Gotta admit, you surprised me."

"Shane, I—"

He gave her a look that made the words die on her tongue. Not so much hard as pleading, although there was a touch of steel in his blue eyes, telling her he was about to clam up. He didn't want to talk about a situation that hurt, and she needed to stop pushing.

She lifted her hands in a gesture of surrender. "I'm sorry."

He reached out for her, ran a hand over her upper arm. "Don't be." He moistened his lips. "There are just other things I'd rather dwell on."

He was still working on losing out to Cal Llewelyn. He must have loved the woman he lost very much. Probably still had strong feelings for her.

And she was good with that.

Wasn't she?

Chapter Eleven

SHANE COULDN'T GET Cal Llewelyn out of his head…or rather he couldn't get the conversation he'd had with Ella over the matter out of his head. The transparency of his reaction to her question disturbed him. Hell, he might as well have worn a sign that said, "Still not over it." He was. The Darcy part anyway.

He cleared his throat as he unrolled a length of bright orange flagging.

"Sorry I got bent out of shape by your question earlier. The one about Cal." Shane tied the flagging around a post that needed to be replaced. Zach had suggested that the two summer hires could replace the rotting wooden posts and Shane hadn't fought him. He'd find the posts; they'd replace them with new treated posts. Ella had come along for the ride. They had two more days together and he didn't want to make them unpleasant for her by acting like a jerk. And the truth was, he was embarrassed about his response to her question about Cal, embarrassed by his lack of cool.

"I totally get it." There was a measure of sincerity in her

voice that made him believe her. "I didn't realize the magnitude of the question. I thought, since he was here on the ranch and friendly with your brother, that you guys had gotten into some kind of a pissing match over some matter of honor, and I was curious as to what it was. I never dreamed…I mean, like I said, he and Zach seemed fine."

"Yeah. Well, he was our CPA for several years before he got engaged to Darcy. It isn't like we should take away our account for that. They weren't sneaking around behind my back or anything. They got together a couple months after we broke up."

Which made the time frame even smaller, which, in turn would make Ella wonder what Darcy saw in Cal that she didn't see in Shane. Something that made her agree to marry him in a very short amount of time.

"Hey," he said softly, leaning on the post to take the pressure off his knee, and hoping he wasn't being too obvious about it. "Let me make this right. We can go into Marietta after work. Have dinner or something."

"Like a date?"

"Uh…yes?" He liked her. He wanted to wine and dine her while they were together. Being with Ella made his brain feel as good as his body—when she wasn't asking uncomfortable questions about issues he was still dealing with. Under different circumstances, in which she didn't have places to go, things to achieve, and he knew what he wanted to be when he grew up, he might have wined and dined her in a serious way. This wasn't the time—not even close to the time, when he might be where he wanted to be.

"Do you know what I would really like?"

"What's that?"

"Picnic by the river." When he frowned at her, she explained, "We have a river running through the ranch in Nevada. We're pretty lucky in that; however, it's not a friendly river. The current is slow and muddy in the summer and it's a raging torrent in the spring." She smiled at him. "Your river is beautiful. I'd like to go wading. Get my feet wet."

"I could take you to the swimming hole."

"You've got an honest-to-goodness swimming hole?"

"Well, kind of."

She didn't ask for more of an explanation, and she didn't get one until later that day, after they'd finished marking posts, and had gone home to shower and see what Zach—who was at the rodeo board meeting—had in the fridge. Shane packed a cooler and the two of them set off for the river, driving the UTV across the pasture to the west side, where the family had fenced off a stretch of river so that the cows didn't muck it up.

"It's gorgeous," Ella said after he'd taken her hand and led her to the place where he and his brothers had played as kids. There was no tire swing, because there'd been no tree large enough to support one back in the day, but, other than that, it was a classic swimming area in the deep bend of an oxbow where the water didn't flow.

"It's not as deep as it once was. Dad used to dig it out for us every year with the excavator. Zach tried to do it the summer after Dad died and made a mess of it. The next year he tried again, and did a decent job, but..." Shane swallowed as emotions he thought were long dealt with welled up "...after losing Dad, none of us spent much time swimming. It was like we suddenly had the need to be grown-up thrust upon us. Life changed. I got into junior rodeo. Cody focused on his motorcycles and cars. Zach became Zach. And we all pitched in together on the ranch."

"How old were you when your dad died?"

"I was six. Cody was eleven." He hadn't had a lot to offer in the way of ranch work at that age, but he'd learned fast. Grew up driving a tractor and baling hay. Moving cattle from pasture to pasture, pushing them through the chutes on branding day. He'd grown into job after job. One reason his brothers had agreed to him disappearing for long stretches during the rodeo season when they could use him on the ranch was because he'd lost Dad so early. It was a concession to the time they'd had with him that Shane had not.

"Big age spread between you guys."

"Mom had trouble with her pregnancies. After me, they stopped. No girl for Mom." Cody used to try to tease him by telling him that their mom finally got her girl, but his mom was enough of a cowhand that Shane hadn't taken it as an insult. "She finally got a couple girls—stepdaughters after remarrying. She lives in Washington now."

"Do you see her often?"

"She's really busy with high-school-aged kids, but we get together when we can."

"I bet you that she found three boys were easier to raise than two girls."

"I don't know. She put up with enough crap from us. Even after the bad thing happened." He put his thumb and forefinger beneath Ella's chin and lifted. "Sorry to be a downer."

"It's not a downer, Shane. It's life. You guys came through it." She pulled in a breath, worked up a smile. "You did good."

Shane stabbed the toe of his boot into the sand. If he'd done good, then why didn't he have anything to show for it?

Lack of planning. He'd let years slip by, never giving much thought to the future, because no matter what, he had a roof over his head. Food to eat. A pickup to drive. The ranch bought everything, which made it essentially impossible for him to leave the ranch without starting over from scratch.

Not that he was leaving. He loved the ranch, couldn't imagine living elsewhere.

"I'd say a penny for your thoughts, but I'm afraid to after last time."

He looked up at her, let fly with the first thing that came to mind. "How'd you know what you wanted to do with your life, Ella?"

She gave a small laugh. "I was *so* certain of what I wanted to do when I first headed to college, but now that I've finished two degrees and am starting another, I find that I'm not as certain as I once was. That's why this master's is going to be in a different field."

Two degrees and working on another. A master's.

Hearing those words was like cold water dripping on the back of his neck, emphasizing how far apart they were in so many respects.

"Hey," she said softly. He glanced up from the river. "You're looking serious."

He shook his head, forced a tight-lipped smile. It became more genuine as she took a sauntering step forward and ran a light hand up his chest to curl over his shoulder. She was so damned beautiful, and easy to be around—even when she was talking about stuff he wasn't comfortable with.

"You make me realize how fortunate I am to still have both parents. We talked a lot about the future and schooling and they gave me good advice."

Shane exhaled deeply and put an arm around her waist, pulling her close and holding her against him in a loose embrace as he breathed in the flowery smell of her hair. If she wanted to think it was lack of parenting that led him to his current point in life, so be it. Zach had told him to finish school. He'd chosen not to, because, hey, when you're not quite twenty, your future stretches on forever. Lots of time to make something of yourself. Right?

Ella tilted her head back to smile up at him. "You should take those boots off. Get your feet wet."

"Just the boots?"

Her eyebrows lifted. "I will not stop you if you remove more than the boots."

A slow smile curved his lips. "Yeah. I won't fight you on that one either."

Ella stepped back and pulled her shirt up over her head and dropped it on the blanket Shane had spread on the grass after they'd arrived. He did the same. Their gazes remained locked on one another as they slowly disrobed, Shane following Ella's lead. When they'd shucked out of everything, he held out a hand and she took it, allowing him to lead her to the bank and then down into the water. She let out a blissful sigh. "This is so great!"

"Your river back home isn't a skinny-dipping river?"

"Well, I'm not saying we haven't done that, but the window of opportunity is small."

"Somewhere between mud and torrent?"

"Exactly." She stepped closer, sliding her hands around his waist, and despite the effect of the cold water, Shane's body instantly responded. He pulled her closer, then kissed her hard, all the frustration of being where he was in his life, and not where he wanted to be due to his own lack of planning, welling up as his dick grew even harder. Ella did not seem to mind. She fisted her hands in the back of his hair, holding his head as she met his kiss and made some demands of her own. The fierceness of her response surprised him. He started to scoop her up in his arms, but lurched sideways as his shoulder gave him a sharp warning and his knee started to give. No scooping. Instead he broke the kiss, took her hand and led her back to the blanket and laid her down. Damned knee and shoulder.

But all thought of injury and abilities left his brain as he stretched his body out along hers, took her mouth in another hard kiss. Ella pushed him onto his back without breaking the kiss, rolled on top of him. His hands skimmed over her curves down to her ass, which he pressed against his hard-on, thrusting against her as she pressed back.

When she ended the kiss and pushed herself upright, she was breathing hard. Long black hair spilled over her shoulders onto his chest in a sheet of silk. "I'm going to fuck you, Shane."

The announcement was unnecessary, and maybe the hottest thing he'd heard in forever.

"Yeah." He managed to get the word out. "I think you should do that."

And fuck him she did. Taking her time, slowing down, challenging him to hold off when he got too close. Then she'd start riding him again, slowly, slowly, until she finally got too close to hold off. He could see her trying, see her throat move as she swallowed after coming to a sharp stop, then she started to seriously move, a cry rising in her throat.

He didn't hear it because his own body exploded, and he made a low guttural sound of his own as he wrapped his arms around her.

Ella collapsed onto his sweat-slicked chest, panting close to his ear—the best sound ever. A few seconds later she rolled off him and cast her gaze toward the river.

"I'm going to take that dip now."

He smiled a little. "I'll join you." He pushed to his feet, then held a hand out for Ella. She took it and allowed him to heft her up.

"You almost went down earlier," she murmured as they walked hand in hand to the river. "When you tried to pick me up."

"Yeah. Not to be cliché, but the brain was writing checks the body couldn't cash."

They waded out waist deep, then stood facing each other in the clear river water. Ella's expression grew thoughtful. "I don't think you should ride with your knee and shoulder like they are. You're going to beat yourself to death."

"I'm riding."

Ella splashed water up her arms, then glided out toward the slow current in a sidestroke. "Would it matter if you missed one rodeo? Took an extra week to heal before your hometown rodeo? I know how much that one means to you."

They'd talked about the Copper Mountain Rodeo the night before, he and Ella and his brothers, sharing stories.

Funny how many firsts in their lives were tied to that rodeo.

Shane stayed where he was, curling his toes into the smooth pebbles and sand beneath his feet. "Yeah. It would. I need to make the finals, but more than that, I need to finish first in the points."

"You don't have to be first to make finals."

"There's a bonus at the end of the season for the top bareback bronc rider. The B.B. Gilmore Award, named after—"

"The legendary Montana bareback rider. He was just finishing his career when Mitch was a senior, also riding bareback." She reversed course and swam back toward him. "How much of a bonus?"

"Enough to pay for some job training so that I have something to fall back on." He only wished he had a clue what that might be. Something that he could do in a rural area. That was his only parameter, although he wouldn't mind what as long as it was something he actually liked to do. But right now he had to tell the beautiful woman who was starting to mean so much to him the cold, hard truth. "Ella…I own a truck and a saddle. I have no training and in a few months, I'll have no occupation, except as a ranch hand."

"You don't own part of your family ranch?"

"Are you familiar with the concept of land rich, cash poor?" He might have a great inheritance to pass on to his kids, but owning the ranch was like owning a piece of the moon. He couldn't sell it, so it was simply a place to live and work. "I want to be able to support myself without depending only on the ranch."

"Admirable goal," Ella said softly as she came to stand where she'd been before she'd started swimming, water sheeting off her naked breasts, dripping off her hair. She looked like a freaking river nymph. If he wasn't so damned spent, if she hadn't wrung everything out of him, he would have tried to carry her out of the river again.

"Is it worth destroying yourself?" she asked softly, jarring him back to the matter at hand. "There must be other ways."

"I'm going with the quick route." It was the only path he had that would allow him to achieve his goal in a reasonable time frame.

Ella lifted a hand to smooth back his hair, but she didn't say anything. Instead she kissed him—a slow, sweet kiss that told him she understood what he'd just told her—that he needed to build something that was his own, and not simply ride on his brothers' coattails. Especially now that he would no longer be rodeoing. When rodeo ended, his identify, the thing that made him different than his older brothers, also ended. Shane Marvell, ex-rodeo rider…that wasn't going to get him anything, except maybe a free drink at Grey's if the owner was in a good mood—which he rarely was.

Shane needed a new identity. A new life. Then maybe he'd be in a place to build something with a woman like Ella.

A WINDSTORM SHOOK the trailer as Ella tried to sleep. If the wind hadn't kept her awake, then thoughts of Shane would have. Being with him felt so ridiculously natural. Was it because they'd had sex before the tenth date? Was that why she felt connected to him in a way she'd never been before with anyone this early in a relationship?

One particularly heavy blast of wind brought her upright, half afraid that the roof would peel off the trailer, then she laid her head back down when the trailer stopped shaking. Shane's scent was on the pillow and when she closed her eyes, it was easy to imagine that he was there. He could have been there. He offered. She wasn't yet ready to share a bedroom with him in the small house with his brothers, so he suggested that he sleep in the trailer with her. As much as she would have loved to fall asleep in his arms, she wasn't ready to do that. As it was, his brothers suspected there was something between them, but had no real proof. She figured if they slept apart, then Shane wouldn't be peppered with questions when she left. His brothers would have theories and guesses as to what their relationship was and nothing more.

When she emerged from the trailer the next morning, she had to step over the branches that littered the ground between the trailer and the house. The old trees had taken a beating.

Shane was on his way out the door as she approached, and he held open the screen, then followed her back into the house.

"I was just coming out to see you. The shower is free."

He'd sent a text during the night, asking if she wanted to share a bed during the storm, but as tempting as the offer was, she'd declined. They'd spent their days together and she told herself that was enough for a summer adventure—at least while they were on his home turf with relatives close by.

"Excellent."

When Ella emerged from the bathroom a half hour later, Shane had a cup of coffee waiting for her.

"A neighbor spotted some of our cattle in his fields. The wind must have blown a branch onto the fence and you know how cows are."

"They can sense a hole in a fence from a mile away?"

Shane smiled at her over his coffee cup, their gazes connecting in a way that made her feel like crossing the kitchen and jumping him. But Zach was in the office and there would be no kitchen jumping.

"Len and Kerry are gathering the cattle. I'm going to look for the hole in the fence. Want to come?"

Ella smiled. "Yes."

"On horseback?"

Her smile widened. "Double yes."

Shane set his cup aside and crossed the kitchen to kiss her lightly on the lips. "Then I'll catch a few horses."

Ella also put her cup aside, but resisted the temptation to settle her hands at his waist. Even with Zach there, it was very possible that one thing would lead to another, and then who would ride that fence? "I'll help you."

"Great. Breakfast?"

"Energy bar?" She patted her soft-sided bag that had a little of everything in it—her toothbrush, a book to read, snacks for emergencies.

"I do love a woman who's ready for anything."

Ella's stomach did a funny little flip, but she casually pushed her damp braid over her shoulder and said, "Kind of the Etch family credo. I was the only slacker."

Shane shook his head. "I don't think so."

"What do you mean?"

"I think it's a matter of degree. You might be the most cautious lion, but you're still a lion and a hell of a lot scarier than, say, an antelope."

Ella's eyebrows lifted. "Is that a compliment?"

"It's a poor analogy, but you are gutsier than a lot of people I know, including a few rodeo guys. They're ropers, of course, but, hey—" he smiled crookedly "—you know."

Ella laughed. "Give me a few minutes to get my boots and a coat and I'll be right with you."

ELLA AND SHANE rode two of the ranch colts destined for the ranch horse sale in October as they set out along the fence line—both quiet horses that showed a lot of promise. The Marvell ranch was known for their colts, thanks to their trainer, Jason Mann, who was helping his wife's family on the Marvell North for a few weeks. Shane had a feeling that Jason and Meg might eventually move to the North ranch permanently, which would leave them in need of a horse trainer. Shane and Cody were adequate, but Jason had a gift. Shane hated to see Jason go, but he now understood doing what you had to do for the woman you love.

When they reached the pasture the cows had escaped from, there were only two fence lines that could have been breached—the north and east. They were currently on the west, which was longer, but less likely to have a hole due to the lack of trees.

Shane pulled his horse to a stop near the gate, then leaned down to unlatch it and let it swing open. He was feeling a little creaky, but overall, his shoulder was showing signs of recovery and his knee was a hell of a lot less swollen. Riding hurt a little, but nothing like it would have when he'd had to have Ella drive him to the ranch. Maybe he still did have the capability to bounce back.

Ella rode through after him, then maneuvered her horse to close the gate again. Jason had done a good job with the colts. Both performed their end of the job perfectly.

"Tell you what," Shane said, resting his hands on the saddle horn. "Why don't you ride the east fence and I'll cut cross-country to the northwest corner, then ride back along the north boundary and meet you."

"Sure." She leaned a hand back on the rump of her

horse, making him wish he'd had a phone to take a photo so he could remember her like this, dressed in old jeans and a denim jacket, a green wild rag bringing out the hints of evergreen in her hazel eyes. The flat hat that had caught his attention many rodeos ago fastened under her chin with a braided stampede string, her long black braid hanging over one shoulder. As at home on a horse as any of the ranch hands.

Shane cleared his throat. "If you encounter any trouble..."

She grinned. "What? Yell?"

He dug into his saddlebag and handed her a pistol, butt first. "Fire a shot. I'll come running."

She cocked her head. "What if you get into trouble?"

"I'll scream like a little girl and you come running."

She laughed and turned to put the pistol in her saddlebags. "Deal."

Shane turned his horse and started toward the far corner of the pasture, his horse leaving the other without any kind of a tussle. Good colts this year.

He trotted the distance to the edge of the meadow, then slowed to a walk before heading through a wide belt of trees, emerging into a high meadow, then back into the trees. Limbs lay everywhere, but his colt picked his way around them. Ella would have fewer trees, fewer branches to deal with. He figured he'd be able to check the entire northern boundary, then turn the corner to the east and meet her about a quarter of the way down that fence line. Then they could share findings, make a battle plan.

And he also had to plan for after Red Rock. What then?

He hadn't expected to start feeling so attached to Ella. So attuned to everything about her. He assumed she'd head back to Nevada to her studies. He'd make some hard life choices of his own. And then?

Nothing.

Try as he might, he couldn't picture how they could hook up again, living such different lives, which made him all the more determined to enjoy the time he did have with Ella.

He found the hole about a quarter of a mile from the boundary corner. An older bug-ravaged fir tree had snapped, coming down on the fence. He managed to drag it free and make a quick fix with the tools he had in his saddlebags by snipping a length of wire from the bottom strand. A calf might go under, but it'd make its way back as calves tended to do.

Mounting again was a painful process, but thankfully the colt tolerated him climbing aboard on the wrong side. Time to hook up with Ella, head home. He'd just rounded the corner and was starting down the east side when he heard not a pistol shot, but a scream. A long, loud scream that made the hair rise on the back of his neck.

Shit.

He urged the colt forward down the slope into a gully,

then back up the other side. He crested the hill in time to see Ella's rider-less horse disappearing into the edge of the trees at a dead run.

"Ella!"

"Shane!"

It took a few seconds, but he spotted her wedged into the fork of a gnarly aspen tree.

"Be careful," she called to him. "There's a bear!"

No further explanation needed. Keeping his eye peeled for signs of cubs, and wishing like hell that his pistol wasn't on its way back to the ranch, he moved the colt forward. The horse's ears were pricked forward and he snorted as bear smell reached his nostrils.

The bear was apparently long gone, and by the time he reached the tree and dismounted, Ella was gingerly working her way down. She stumbled as her boots hit the ground, then caught her balance. Her eyes were wide, her face pale as she started toward him. Her hat was on her back, held there by the stampede string.

"We don't have bears in Nevada," she said in a shaky voice.

Shane wrapped his arms around her, nestling her head under his chin as he searched the underbrush for signs of movement. She was shaking, and he didn't blame her one bit.

"It came up out of that gully, snorting and grunting. Scared the hell out of my horse. He knocked me off on the tree limb."

Shane drew back and brushed the hair off Ella's forehead. Sure enough, there was the beginnings of a bruise blooming there. "I'm so sorry, kid."

Ella gave a shudder as she let out a long breath. "I'm okay. The tree was a blessing and a curse. I might still be on if it hadn't been there. But if I hadn't been able to stay on top, then I wouldn't have had anything to climb."

"What did the bear look like?"

"Scary."

"Big? Small? Black? Blond?"

She shook her head. "Its nose was browner than the rest of it."

"Probably a black bear. Which is better than having a grizzly on the property."

"Normally I'd apologize for being such a wuss, but I'm not going to. That bear was terrifying."

As was getting knocked off her horse and not knowing if she was about to be attacked. Shane ran a soothing hand over her back, wishing like hell that he'd been there. There was nothing he could do to make things better, except to be here for her now.

"Maybe we can get out of here," Ella said against his shirt, even though she showed no other signs of wanting to leave his arms.

He jerked his head toward the colt. "Let's see if Jason prepped this guy to ride double."

"What if we get dumped and the bear comes back?"

"We find another tree." Shane smiled down at her. "But the bear is probably long gone. Unless you threaten her food source or her cubs, she's going to leave us be."

Ella let out another shaky breath, then stepped back. Shane cupped her cheek with his palm, stared down into her pale face. He hated that he'd accidentally put her in danger, hated that he hadn't been there when she'd needed him.

And more than that, he hated that he couldn't tell her just how much he was coming to care for her.

ELLA'S HEART RATE still wasn't normal by the time they got to the ranch, but riding behind Shane had made her feel slightly more secure.

It was not knowing what was going to happen after she'd hit the ground that had been the most frightening. Her brain had gone into primal survival mode after she'd landed, and, assuming attack was imminent, she'd instinctively raced to the tree and started to climb, her boots fouling her up as she attempted to get purchase on the slick bark. By sheer willpower, it seemed, she'd made her way up the tree to the high fork in time to see the bear snuffle and grunt its way back into the underbrush.

And then Shane had yelled.

She could say with all honesty that she'd never been so glad to see anyone in her entire life. Glad and then terrified that he, too, would be attacked.

Although…the bear hadn't attacked. The bear had scared the shit out of her horse and the colt had run under the branch, knocking her to the ground before she'd gotten control.

An unexpected shudder went through her, and Shane gave her a concerned look over his shoulder.

"I'm fine," she muttered. "Just trying to convince myself I'm a lion and not an antelope."

Shane gave a low laugh and she felt better. A couple minutes later, she dismounted from behind him and opened the gate leading to the ranch. Her legs felt shaky, but it also felt good to walk the last little bit to the hitching post where Shane dismounted. His knee buckled a little, but after their talk at the river, she refrained from making comment.

"Your horse," he said pointing at the corral where the sweat-drenched bay colt she'd been riding was pacing the fence.

Ella was about to say, "Thank goodness," when a voice came from behind them. "What the hell happened?"

They turned together to see Zach heading toward them from the direction of the tack shed.

"I was about to head out to find you."

"A bear," Shane said. "Ella got knocked off by a low branch when the colt bolted."

"Are you okay?" Zach asked as he came to a stop next to Shane's horse.

"Fine." Ella faked a smile. Shane shifted his weight, but didn't rat her out. Yes, she had a contusion and she'd get some ice on it, but she was embarrassed enough as it was and didn't need to be fussed over. Not that Zach looked like a fusser. "Thanks for taking care of my horse."

"Not a problem." Zach shot a look at Shane that Ella couldn't read. "Did you find the hole?"

"Found and temporarily fixed."

"Good. Len and Kerry should be back with the cattle anytime now."

"They can turn them into the pasture they came out of."

Zach gave a nod and headed toward the shop without another word.

"Thanks, again," Ella called after him. He raised a hand, then continued on.

Ella turned back to Shane who'd started uncinching the saddle. "Sorry to give your brother a scare."

"He's been through worse," Shane said dryly. He didn't argue when Ella took hold of the heavy saddle and dragged it off. She lugged it to the tack shed, and when she came back out after depositing it on an empty rack, he was standing next to the door, holding the colt by the reins.

Truthfully, she was still shaken. And just as truthfully, she didn't want him to know that.

But he did.

Without a word he reached out to slide his hand around her neck, his expression intent as he pulled her closer, not for a kiss, but to bring her against his body, hold her against him with one arm tightly clamped around her waist. She melted in to him, sought comfort, something she was never good at doing. But it felt right to draw strength from Shane and she had the oddest feeling that he was doing the same with her.

They stood for the longest time, until the colt pawed the ground and blew out an impatient breath, sprinkling moisture over Ella's arm.

"Yuk." She shook off her arm, then wiped it on her jeans before making a face at Shane. "Horse snot."

He laughed, but his heart wasn't in it. He was somewhere else in his head, thinking who knew what. Whatever it was, it involved her, and it was deeper than a fun summer fling.

"Stop thinking," she said.

A startled expression crossed his face. "Excuse me?"

Ella pressed her lips together briefly. "I have one more day on the ranch with you before we head back to real life."

"You want to hold real life at bay?" he asked in a low voice.

She slid her arms up around his neck and ignored the colt nuzzling her shoulder.

"Yes, please. One more day."

Chapter Twelve

"YOU HAVEN'T CALLED Dr. Bruch back?" Avery leaned across the picnic table Ella and Jenna shared. The Red Rock rodeo would commence that evening and, after driving up with Shane, she'd kissed him, then left him to stretch and prepare mentally while she hooked up with her friends for lunch at the picnic tables next to the concession stand.

"No. I did call him."

"I mean the second time."

"I'm holding off until after the Copper Mountain Rodeo." The rodeo Shane was so looking forward to, for reasons other than competition. He and his brothers truly loved the event.

"Why?" Jenna asked.

"I'd say the answer is obvious," Avery replied without looking at her sister. "Ella is weighing possibilities."

Ella sucked a breath in between her teeth. "Exactly." If only she had more information to make an informed decision. That was why she was waiting. She knew the best path for her security-wise. It was clear and direct and all it would take was a phone call to land a position with one of Dr. Bruch's associates, who had an open internship. Making that phone call was a no-brainer...except that Ella couldn't bring herself to do it. She told herself it was because if she did, she'd be locking into studying adolescent responses to academic stress when she really wanted to study risk behaviors in rodeo competitors, but that wasn't the full truth.

"You want to stay in Montana."

"Until I figure out a few things, yes."

Avery didn't bother to ask what those things were. "Do you want to stay with us?"

"I don't know," Ella said honestly. If she did, she'd get a job in Dillon. Pay her way. It was an easy drive from Dillon to Marietta. Under three hours.

The idea of doing something out of the ordinary for more than a summer was both scary and exciting. The fact that excitement was stronger than fear told her that she wasn't ready to go back to Reno, lock herself into a course of study and a job. Her adventure wasn't over, yet.

Avery leaned back against the booth cushion. "Do you have any kind of a game plan?"

"Yes." Ella gave a quick nod. "I will eat my guts out, then make a decision after the Copper Mountain Rodeo." Actually, she planned to try very hard *not* to agonize and to instead let her instincts take over. New territory for her. She wasn't being impulsive so much as she wasn't going to die the coward's thousand deaths.

She hoped.

"Good for you." Jenna gave Ella's hand a reassuring pat. "Your crazy family will be proud."

"Oddly," Ella said before taking a sip of her Coke, "they seem kind of worried." At least Finley had been when Ella had explained the situation, which made her wonder why they all thought she was such a snowflake. An Etch family variety of a snowflake, she amended, remembering what Shane had said about things being relative. She might be a lion, like the rest of them, but they pretty much considered her a cowardly lion.

"You just show them," Jenna said bracingly. She glanced down at her phone as a text came in and smiled. "I'm going out for drinks with a bull rider tonight."

"If he's ambulatory," Avery added dryly.

"Who?" Ella asked.

Color rose in Jenna's cheeks. "T.J."

Ella gave a small laugh. "You won't have to worry about making conversation. T.J. will do that for you."

Avery nodded her agreement before taking a big bite of her neglected hamburger and Jenna beamed.

"Good. I'm supposed to see him before he goes behind the chutes to firm things up." She reached down for her purse. "So I should go and, you know...firm things up."

"Check your look." Avery lifted her chin. "You can borrow anything of mine you want."

"Thanks." Jenna slid clear of the table and dumped the remains of her late lunch in the trash barrel.

"She'll wear a white shirt and jeans," Avery said with a rueful shake of her head as Jenna disappeared into the maze of trucks and trailers behind them.

"She looks good in simple stuff," Ella replied.

"But she doesn't turn heads."

"She'll turn the right head. And in the meantime, she can hang with T.J."

THE ARENA STARTED to clear as the warm-up ended, riders exiting under the archway as the tractor began to make its final pass to smooth the ground prior to the first event. Shane's event.

Shane worked one side of his rigging as Tyson worked the other until they were both satisfied that the Barstow was secure.

"It's good," Tyson muttered. Shane nodded and Tyson headed to the man gate.

Shane let out a breath and ran a hand over the horse's neck, dragging his fingers through the mane before stepping back to lace up his glove.

He was doing his damnedest to concentrate on the matter at hand, but it wasn't taking. He, who had laser focus before a ride, could not move beyond the fact that Ella was thinking of giving up her studies—and a way to pay for them—to stay in Montana. He had T.J. to thank for passing along the gossip almost as soon as he'd heard it from Jenna Glenn.

Ella staying in Montana was a situation that had disaster written all over it—he wasn't going to have her making sacrifices that might alter the course of her future to spend more time with him. Especially when he wouldn't be able to measure up.

Having her come to resent him because he was at a dead end would kill him. He needed to prove that he could be more, that he wasn't just a cowboy sharing a house with his brothers…and the truth was, even if he won the bonus money, he didn't know if he could be more. He thought he could, but what if he failed?

Ella, with her college degrees and academic smarts, might be a ranch kid, but she lived in a different reality than he did. She had a future—if she didn't blow it trying to be with him. He'd been on board for a summer romance, because he wouldn't disappoint in that arena, but now, with Ella thinking of pushing the envelope…

Shit. It froze him up inside. How could it not?

"Shane!"

From the clipped note in the chute boss's voice, Shane had the feeling it wasn't the first time the guy had said his name as he pulled his rigging.

"Yeah."

"Order's been changed. You'll buck second."

"Got it." Shane wiggled his fingers in the thick glove, checked the lace again, then leaned against the rail as the grand entry began, closed his eyes and visualized his ride.

You've got this. The only thing that matters is the here and now. The ride.

He breathed in deeply. Exhaled.

Wished like hell that he could believe his own mantra.

RED ROCK WAS a smaller venue than most, and despite taking place on a Monday and Tuesday, it was a popular one due to its rough-and-tumble, no-frills reputation. Nothing made rich people come out in force like the opportunity to pretend they didn't like coddling, so the stands were packed. Ella adjusted her position, wishing she'd tried to find a place at the crowded rail, but it was too late now. The rodeo was about to begin and she didn't want to miss Shane's ride. After the ride, if all went well, of course—which it would—she would talk to Shane. Tell him the things she hadn't told him on the two-hour drive to Red Rock, because she didn't want to distract him before the rodeo.

He cared for her. She was certain of that. Their summer adventure was blossoming into something more, and she wasn't going to simply walk away, head back to Reno, even if she now had something to go back to. Several months ago, she would have done that, because plans were made and she always followed through, regardless of personal cost.

Ella sucked in her breath as a woman squeezed by her,

almost banging her in the face with a giant purse, then lifted her chin as she spotted Cody Marvell close to the entry gate. She apologized to the person next to her and got to her feet, squeezing by to get to the stairs leading down from the stands. She'd watch with Cody.

She'd just made it around the ticket booth when the first bronc ride began. She stopped and watched as the cowboy rode a snorting gelding to the six- or seven-second mark before flying off and landing hard on his shoulder.

Bad luck that. Ella pulled in a breath and hurried on.

The announcer directed the crowd to turn their attention to chute number five so that they could watch the top bareback bronc rider in the state of Montana just as Ella dodged around a horse and eased up to Cody's side. He gave her a startled look, then smiled broadly.

"Hey," he said, stepping aside to give her some room.

"Hey," she replied, keeping her eyes on the arena. "I escaped the stands when I saw you. Hope you don't mind."

"Not at—"

He stopped speaking as the gate opened and Shane's horse reared out of the gate. Ella could tell the second he marked the bronc out that something was off. Two seconds in, the bronc spun one way and Shane went the other. He hit the dirt on his good shoulder, then Ella gasped and recoiled as the horse threw a sharp kick at Shane's head. Shane threw himself back into the dirt a split second before the hoof made contact, then slowly climbed to his feet as the announcer offered his condolences from up in the booth. The audience paid Shane off with a rousing burst of applause as he limped to the gate.

Ella blinked a couple times, realizing then that there were tears trickling down her face. Cody took hold of her arm.

"Are you okay?"

"Yeah." The word came out automatically as she wiped her cheeks with the back of her hand.

"I don't think so."

Ella cleared her throat, wiped one more time. "Reaction. My brother got kicked in the head. He's okay, but he still has some memory issues."

"No, shit," Cody said, letting go of her arm.

"We thought he was going to die. It was touch and go."

"Yet you follow the rodeo."

She attempted a smile, embarrassed at her knee-jerk response to Shane's near miss, but it fell flat and she gave up, sensing that Cody was no easier to bullshit than Shane was. "My brother told me it wasn't about dying. It was about living. It was hard to accept, but I finally realized that you can't stop people from doing what they love." So instead she tried to find out *why* they did what they did. "And…things will happen whether I'm here or not."

Cody gave a considering nod. "I guess they will." He jerked his head toward the trailers. "Shall we go see him?"

"Yeah."

"He'll be in a mood."

Ella smiled a little. This time for real. "I can take it."

SHANE WAS UNTYING the laces around his ankles that kept his boots from flying off during a ride when he saw Ella and Cody approaching the truck. He hadn't expected Cody to attend the rodeo, mainly because his brother hadn't said one word about going. Yet here he was—with Ella, no less. He hadn't seen her since they parted company after arriving in Red Rock, and it was kind of crazy how T.J.'s teasing tidbit of gossip had shifted his perspective. But shift it, it did.

Ella was *not* going to freaking give up anything for him. Wasn't going to happen. He would not be put in a position where he had to disappoint yet another good woman. And because of that, his expression was grimmer than he intended when he made eye contact with her, and then his mouth hardened even more.

Damned if she hadn't been crying. He could see telltale tracks at the corners of her eyes. It better not have been over him. His gut tightened. Not good that he wanted to pull her against him, tell her he was fine and make it all right.

The best way he could make things all right was by making certain they abided by the agreement they started with.

"I know you don't like to talk after you fuck up," Cody said, "but I stopped on my way to the Marvell North to watch you ride." He tilted his head at Ella. "And I had a witness to being here, so I could either swear her to secrecy or stop and tell you I've seen you do better."

"Thanks," Shane said darkly. His brother was correct—he did not like to talk after fucking up. "Why are you heading north?"

"To pick up Jason. Meg's staying and needs the truck. I told him I'd make the trip because those colts aren't going to train themselves for the ranch horse sale."

"You guys coming straight back?"

"ASAP. Having Jason back will take off some of the pressure on the ranch."

Pressure that he added to by having this last season. Well, he'd soon be there full time, doing his part with the rest of the crew.

Cody talked for a few more minutes about the trip ahead of him as silent tension grew in the small trailer, then, after bouncing a puzzled glance between Shane and Ella, he said he needed to be going if he was going to hit Sweetheart, the closest town to the Marvell North, before midnight.

After Cody closed the trailer door behind him, Ella met Shane's gaze, but it took her a few seconds to say, "Sorry about your ride."

"It happens. I'm high enough in the points I can take a loss." One to be exact. He had to excel at the Copper Mountain Rodeo next week to make up for it.

"So…you're okay?"

Yeah, I am. Why were you crying?

Maybe it was best he didn't know. "I'm okay."

Shane had no idea how to dive into what he had to say next, or whether this was even the time *to* dive in. Would later be better? He couldn't see how. He'd always pulled his Band-Aids off quickly, and later would mean at the next rodeo.

"What are you going to do now?" Ella finally asked.

"I'm heading home, Ella." He hadn't made the short go, so there was no sense in hanging around.

"I…uh…could spare some days. Come with you." She must have read something in his expression, because her fine dark brows drew together. "Or not."

"I heard that you're giving up the internship." He'd meant to speak casually, but the words came out sounding like an accusation.

Ella gave him a perplexed look, then her expression changed as she apparently followed some trail of logic to T.J. "What of it?"

"You can't do that."

"Why not?" The words dropped like stones.

"Let me rephrase. You can't do that if you're doing it for me."

Her full lips flattened into a surprisingly hard line. "Maybe I'm doing it for me."

"Would you do it if we hadn't been spending so much time together?"

"Sleeping together you mean?"

"And spending time." Even now, when he was trying to

argue her to a place of safety, he couldn't let her think their relationship had been just sex. They were not fuck buddies. He knew they weren't, because he'd had fuck buddies before Darcy. This thing with Ella was nothing close to those relationships. That was why he was so freaking afraid of forever disappointing her with his sad reality.

That was why he was doing what he had to do.

"Ella—"

"Don't you dare say it's been fun."

"I can't have you throwing your internship away. We agreed to be straight with one another."

"You're saying this…" she moved her finger back and forth in the air between them "…thing between us…couldn't turn into anything more."

"Summer adventure, like we said in the beginning. I've loved every minute, but summer's almost over." Her face was growing paler by the minute, but he forged on. "It could end now, or it could end later." His voice softened. "But it's going to end. We're too different, Ella."

She opened her mouth, scowled at him. Closed it again. Then she took a step closer and he steeled himself. "What brought this on, Shane? We were fine this morning and now…this. Is it all because I'm not taking the internship?"

If he went with the truth, if he said, "You can't jeopardize your future for me," she'd fight back. He didn't give her a foothold. "I'm not in a place where I can start a relationship. So I won't."

The words were blunt. Stark. Effective.

She swallowed as she lifted her chin in a gesture that smacked of defiance. "Because of Darcy?"

"Yes." The total truth…only not in the way she thought.

The expression on her face—pain coupled with open regret—destroyed him. He didn't want to hurt her. That was why he was doing what had to be done.

She turned toward the door, but he grabbed her hand. Big mistake, because now that he'd stopped her, he had no idea what to say. So many thoughts crowding into his head. As it turned out, he didn't have to say anything.

"You can't have it both ways." Ella pulled her hand free and reached for the door handle. A second later she was gone.

Not a moment too soon. If losing her now felt this awful, he didn't know how he could have handled it in the future.

~

SHANE WASN'T SURPRISED that the lights were still on in Zach's office when he got home late that night. It wasn't unusual for his brother to fall asleep there. Anyway, Shane hoped he was asleep, because he didn't want to talk about his ride, even if it was just to say he had screwed up. He was hurting on too many levels to not let on that something was amiss, and it probably wouldn't take too much for Zach to figure out that it wasn't the ride.

He hung his hat on one of the hooks next to the door

and then pried his boots off on the iron beetle bootjack before padding through the kitchen in his socks.

He passed the office door on his way down the hall and glanced in to see Zach conked out on the sofa, his long legs stretched out in front of him. Reprieve. It wouldn't last long, though. Tomorrow Cody and Jason would be back and probably one of his brothers would ask about Ella, and he'd say…

He didn't know what he'd say.

Maybe a couple hours' sleep would help his brain function better. He scrubbed a hand over his face as he headed into the bathroom, snapped the light on, then did a double take when he caught sight of his reflection. He looked like hell, all hollow-eyed and grimly serious.

He turned on the water and leaned down to splash some on his face, washing away the arena dust he hadn't bothered with after he and Ella had parted ways. After drying his face, he braced his hands on the sink and let his head hang. He'd done the right thing. The only thing.

It felt worse dumping someone he cared about than it had getting dumped by someone he'd thought he loved. A hell of a lot worse.

He raised his gaze back to the mirror. He'd done it because he did care. And once Ella was back where she belonged, she'd thank him.

Eventually.

When she got done hating on him.

Chapter Thirteen

"YOU'RE NOT COMING home?" Finley's tone was both flat and disbelieving.

Ella swallowed an impatient sigh. "Finn—for the last time—no. I'm not coming home. I'm not taking the internship. I'm staying in Montana."

She'd called Dr. Bruch and thanked him for directing her toward his colleague, then told him that she'd decided to put off pursuing her master's for another year. A year during which she may well be asking about having fries with that, but she didn't care. This journey of hers was not yet done.

Hell—she didn't even know what counted as a destination. She was traveling. Exploring. Experimenting. Doing the stuff she should have done before hyper-focusing on her college degree. And yes, she was still going to ask rodeo riders questions about risk, use the answers to work up a proposal for her master's degree project. But she wasn't going to tackle another degree until she figured out *what* she wanted to do with her life, *where* she wanted to do it and *who* she wanted to do it with.

Her inner voice made a small *ahem* before muttering, *"You know the who."*

All right—she did know the who. She just didn't know if it was possible when Shane had been so adamant about sending her on her way. She had no idea how she'd managed to fall in love with a guy so rapidly, but she had, and analyzing the wherefores and whys wasn't going to change her feelings one bit. When she was with him, she felt whole, and she had a sneaking suspicion that she wasn't alone in her feelings, which begged the question: why did he break it off with her? What was going on?

"That's not a good decision."

Finley was a fine one to talk about bad decisions, and so what if Ella made a few—like everyone else with the Etxeberri surname?

"Have you ever heard of CJ Cooper?" Ella asked.

"Who? No."

"She'd a lady bronc rider I interviewed in July at this little Podunk rodeo. She was working for her pro ticket. She just got it." The Copper Mountain Rodeo would be her first pro ride according to T.J. who seemed to know everything.

"Congrats to her," Finley said dryly.

"And during our interview she said something I think about. She said she didn't want to have regrets because she made her decisions based on what other people might think." Ella had been thinking about that statement more and more over the past several days.

Her sister was unimpressed. "If you're not coming home and you're not going to school, then what *are* you going to do?"

"I'll figure it out."

Ella heard Finley inhale deeply. Then came the exhalation. Long and loud. A sure warning sign, but Ella ignored it.

"Don't even try," she said.

"Try what?" Finley asked darkly.

"To bully me into doing what *you* want me to do."

"Like I would." Finley gave a sniff.

"You guys always used to tease me about being chicken and now this."

"We were talking about rope swings in the barn, not putting your entire life off the rails."

"Finn, I'm twenty-four. I think I will recover if I do screw up."

"Yeah. Like Kadie McGinty?"

"Really?" Kadie McGinty had been valedictorian of Finley's class, won several full-ride scholarships, then eloped with a cowboy on her eighteenth birthday, divorced the guy two years later and had yet to attend a day of college.

"She threw everything away. For a guy. Now you're doing the same."

Ella should have never told Finley about Shane. She hadn't mentioned her feelings, but Finn had put two and two together.

"Let me live my life," Ella said through gritted teeth. "I suffered through all the shit you guys put me through, worrying about river swims and bucking horses and car races and free rock climbs, not to mention that thing you had going with Joshua Crain."

"I knew what I was doing."

"Did you know he'd end up in jail? I did."

"Two years after we broke up."

"The signs were there. He could have stolen those horses years earlier."

Finley did another inhalation, but Ella cut in. "I love you, Finn, but I'm going to do what I want to do. I'll be in touch."

She ended the call and dropped the phone on her chest as she collapsed back against Avery's sofa. Then she picked it back up and turned off the power.

There. That might stop things. At least for a little while.

SHANE HAD TO give Zach credit for not asking about Ella once after his return from Red Rock. Maybe Cody had warned him that something was up, because Cody had also kept his mouth shut about the touchy subject. Or maybe Zach was simply busy with the last-minute details leading up to the 79th Copper Mountain Rodeo. He was in the middle of his first term on the rodeo board, and Shane couldn't help but think that it was good for him to have something to think about other than the ranch—especially if it kept Shane's private life off his brother's radar.

For a while, anyway.

On Thursday, two days before the rodeo, Zach finally broached the subject of Ella.

"What about her?" Shane asked as casually as possible, ignoring the way his gut tightened at her name.

"Will she be at the Copper Mountain Rodeo?" Zach pulled his hat off his head as he stared out over the herd of heifers they'd just moved to the lower pasture, ruffled his damp hair and put the hat back into place. It was freaking hot. The horses were brushed down and hosed off, but Shane and Zach were still sweaty and dirty.

"She's heading back to Nevada. To finish her schooling."

"Nevada's a long way away." Zach continued to study the herd.

"Yeah. All for the best, really." Except for the part where he felt like his heart had been ripped out.

A silence, tenser than it should have been, grew between them until Zach finally shot him a sideways look and said, "You're sure about that?"

So much for not telegraphing. If Zach had picked up on his mood, then he may as well have been wearing a sign.

"Yeah."

Zach turned to lean his arms against the top rail of the lodgepole fence. "Maybe you could explain it to me."

"I have shit to offer her or anyone else, Zach. Cowboy

wages. A bedroom in the main house?"

"Have you hit the point where you have to offer her anything?"

Shane's jaw muscles tightened. "I am never getting to the point where I want to offer something and can't. Better to just end things now."

So they don't end like they did with Darcy. It was beyond easy to read Zach's silent conclusion.

"What's your plan? Are you leaving the ranch?"

"You need me, and I want to be here. But I'm going to get training. I was thinking a mobile welding service, maybe, but I need my certification. If—when—I win the B.B. Gilmore bonus, I want to put it toward tuition. If I have a job, I can make a down payment on a house of some kind. Something bigger than a camp trailer."

"There's always the horse trailer. You won't be using it for rodeo."

It took Shane a moment to realize that his brother was joking. "I guess."

"Where would you put your house?"

Shane gestured to the far end of the pasture with his head. "If you guys agree, I was thinking there by the pine grove. Far enough from the river to not get many mosquitoes, but a ways away from the main ranch."

"If you don't win the bonus, I can front you the money—"

Shane's head jerked around. "No."

Zach's mouth tightened ominously, but he didn't say a word.

"I'll make my own way," Shane muttered before turning to stare back out over the pasture. "There are other ways to save money if I don't win the bonus. It'll just take longer."

He propped his elbows on the top rail, pressed cupped hands against his forehead. "Ella's special, but things were moving fast. Too fast." He had no idea why he was confessing, except that Zach was there and he knew how to keep a secret.

"Kind of scared you."

Shane's hackles started to rise, then fell again as he acknowledged the truth of the simple statement. "After Darcy, yes."

Zach pushed back from the rail, a sign that the conversation was over. "Murphy Stables just bought a load of timothy. I have to see about delivery."

Brotherly guidance and advice—the verbal kind—was done. For now. "I'll do it."

"They'd like it tomorrow."

"I'll deliver it before I head to town for the kick-off events of Rodeo Weekend." The big truck had an automatic transmission, so his knee would be okay.

Zach gave an approving nod. "Glad you're going to the festivities."

"Haven't missed a rodeo since I was four."

"And won the mutton busting."

Dominator had done her best to shake him, but Shane had clung to her back, hanging on to her wool for all he was worth. “One of my more challenging rides.”

Zach laughed, a good sound coming from his serious brother as they fell into step and started for the house, where they’d flip a coin to see who showered first.

Shane glanced over his shoulder at the pine grove. What would it be like to have his own bathroom?

He couldn’t freaking wait to find out.

“Uh…”

Shane glanced over at his brother, who never hesitated when he had something to say.

“I’m glad you decided to go to the festivities willingly.”

“Why’s that?” Shane had a sudden nasty feeling.

“Because I volunteered you to say a few words at the rodeo grounds dedication.”

Shane stopped so quickly that his boots left skid marks in the gravel. “No. Wait. What? *You’re* supposed to say a few words.”

Zach stabbed a finger at him. “But you’re riding in the rodeo. You haven’t missed competing in twenty-two years and would have competed last year if there’d been a rodeo. First sheep, then calves, then broncs. I think the rededication remarks would be better coming from a competitor with such a long record.”

Shane let out a breath. It made sense.

“Fine. I’ll talk. Thirty seconds. And you’ll buy me a bottle of single malt."

Zach smiled. "Small price to pay. And thanks."

"I'M SO GLAD you're coming with us." Jenna reached for the saddle soap and dipped her sponge before going back to work on the breast collar she held on her lap. "I thought that after…" she sucked air through her teeth "…you know…that you'd head back to Nevada."

"Copper Mountain is the next rodeo on the schedule and I'm going," Ella said simply.

Jenna stopped rubbing soap into the breast collar long enough to send Ella an impressed look. The girl had no idea that the information she'd passed along to T.J.—which he, in turn, had passed along to Shane—had precipitated the 'you know.' Or at least that was what Ella had deduced. Her giving up the internship had been front and center in Shane's argument for going their separate ways and that was the only way he could have known so soon after she'd told Avery and Jenna.

He was trying to protect her.

From something.

She was still trying to wrap her brain around what.

"When will you go back?"

"After I settle a few things."

Jenna looked up, but Ella offered no more explanation. She didn't have the details worked out in her head, but she did have an objective.

Jenna put the breast collar aside and reached for her bridle. Ella continued working on the skirts of Avery's saddle. They would leave for Marietta the following morning because according to both Avery and Jenna, Marietta's Copper Mountain Rodeo pre-function was one of the best. They might miss the parade, but they'd be there in time to wander downtown and to attend the picnic in the park.

Would Shane be there?

His ranch was almost an hour away from the town, and being shorthanded, she could see him working through Friday and showing up Saturday for his ride. Was he in any shape to ride?

It didn't matter. He'd ride anyway. He wanted the bonus money and he had the dogged determination that enabled rough-stock riders to push through debilitating pain. Ella was positive he would have ridden through the season even if there was no bonus for top points, because that was what guys like him did.

They were stubborn.

Something she was going to have to deal with.

And deal with it, she would. Because she was a lion, not an antelope.

Chapter Fourteen

AVERY PULLED INTO the competitors' area of the Copper Mountain Rodeo, having charmed her way through the roadblock officials who were setting up for the parade, which ended at the fairgrounds.

"Close one," she said as she found a space to park the micro-trailer between two long aluminum horse trailers. Ella climbed out of the back seat of the truck and stretched her legs.

"This is nice," Jenna said as she surveyed the brand-new facility. The old Copper Mountain Rodeo facility had been destroyed by fire the previous summer and, according to Shane, the locals had pulled together to fundraise and get the new facility built in time for this year's rodeo. They'd done an amazing job, with state-of-the-art bleachers, a roomy announcer's booth, welded rail corrals for the stock.

A marching band started to play, and Avery shot a look over at Ella. "Want to cross the bridge and work our way downtown to watch? Or wait here for the parade to get to us?"

There were already people at the bridge, so Ella said, "Let's wait here. Zach said there would be a dedication ceremony. We can get front-row seats."

As if. But she did want to watch the ceremony. She still didn't know how she was going to handle her first meeting with Shane, but she certainly wasn't going to shy away from any venue where he might be.

Ella, Jenna and Avery grabbed Cokes out of the cooler in the back of the truck, then set their lawn chairs near the bridge. The parade would disperse as it reached the grounds, but they would see the entries as they crossed.

"I love parades," Jenna as she looked back over her shoulder to scan the vehicles parked in the lot around them.

"I thought T.J. wasn't arriving until late."

"You never know," she said, facing forward again and sipping her Coke. Ella fought a smile. Jenna had found a man who loved to talk, so she didn't have to, and T.J. had found a woman who loved to listen. And he was a bull rider.

"If you see Austin Harding, point him out to me," Ella said to Avery. She'd never met the American Extreme Bull Riding alum, but she wanted to. He would be an interesting subject to interview, having gone through several professional tours.

"Will do," Avery said.

"I hope to catch a couple of the other guys I haven't talked to yet. Some of the bronc riders."

"And Shane?"

"Yes." Ella replied without missing a beat. "I hope to catch up to him, too."

And when she did, she was shooting from the hip, trusting that her instincts would guide her through a dicey situation—perhaps the most Etxeberrian things she'd ever done in her life.

The parade was excellent, with creative floats, the local high school band, several kids' groups, and, of course, the horses. Rodeo queens and princesses smiled and waved as they started across the bridge and behind them rode a mounted drill team all decked out in black and silver.

"I would have killed for one of those saddles as a kid," Avery murmured.

Ella laughed. Of course she would have. The saddles were covered in bling.

After the parade, a crowd began to form near the area where the dedication was taking place. Ella, Avery and Jenna stayed where they were, seated in front of their truck. The stage area was quite a distance away, but with the new PA system, they could hear every word of the mic checks.

"We could sneak downtown," Avery said. "Maybe beat the line for those amazing chocolates."

Ella shook her head as she zeroed in on a guy standing near an amazing piece of copper artwork—a life-size bucking horse and cowboy. Her heart gave a kick at the sight of Shane talking to one of the local dignitaries. As much as she'd like an amazing chocolate, there was something in the staging area she wanted a whole lot more.

She moistened her lips, keeping her gaze on Shane as if he would evaporate if she didn't.

"I can catch up with you later."

"Uh…no. I think we'll stay here." Avery stretched her legs out and made a show of getting more comfortable. "Just in case you need backup."

SHANE'S MOUTH WAS dry. He'd already drunk at least a quart of water, but it hadn't helped. He'd never spoken in public before and as he stared out over the people in front of the dedication stands, his insides began to seize up. Again.

Taryn Telford was addressing the crowd and seemed totally at ease. How?

Shane closed his eyes and wished he was about to face the rankest bronc on the planet. It would be a hell of a lot easier than what he was about to do.

"And now, Shane Marvell would like to say a few words."

Shane's eyes snapped open and he got to his feet. Blood pounded in his temples, but amazingly his voice was steady as he said, "Thank you, Taryn."

He looked out over the crowd—friends, neighbors, community members, terrifying people when gathered in a mob like this—and cleared his throat. He was about to launch into his memorized speech—which had kept him up for most of the night, which in turn made him thankful that Zach hadn't sprung this on him any earlier than he had—when he spotted the Glenn sisters' small trailer parked fifty yards away, directly in front of him. And heaven help him, he counted three people sitting in front of the Glenn truck. And judging from the size of those three people, they were all female.

Fuck. Me.

Shane jerked his attention back to the audience and forced a smile, glad he hadn't cursed aloud. "I'm here today to thank everyone for pulling together to get this facility built in time for this year's rodeo. It was a real disappointment when we had to cancel last year, because it was the first time I hadn't ridden some gnarly beast in my hometown in twenty-two years. This is where I got my start, you know, on a sheep named Dominator."

The crowd laughed and Shane began to relax an iota—as much as he could, anyway, while dealing with the possibility that Ella was on the edge of the competitors' lot listening to him.

"This is my last season before I hang up my rigging—" The crowd made an "aww" sound that warmed him inside. "And I'm glad that I'm able to buck here, in my hometown of Marietta. Thank you everyone for making this possible!"

The crowd clapped and there were a few loud whistles and calls of "Good luck, Shane" as he left the stage and went to stand with his brother, who clapped him on the shoulder.

He shot another look at Avery's truck. Still three people there. The third one didn't have to be Ella, but his gut told him it was.

His gut also told him that he had some trouble ahead of him.

"YOU KNOW WHAT?" Ella said to Avery after Shane had made his way offstage. "I do feel like getting chocolate." A *lot* of chocolate. She'd settle her nerves, then…whatever.

Avery patted her knee. "I totally understand."

"Me, too." Jenna scanned the parking lot one more time and after coming up empty, got to her feet. "Let's beat the crowd."

Ella appreciated the fact that her friends didn't make her feel like some kind of a coward because she wasn't yet ready to come face-to-face with Shane, who no doubt thought she was back in Nevada licking her wounds. They made their way across the bridge and walked the short distance to the main street of Marietta, where merchants had set out their wares on tables in front of their stores, and various clubs and groups were manning a variety of booths. There were a few people milling around the displays and perusing the sidewalk sale items, but once the dedication ceremony ended and the crowd left the fairgrounds, Ella had a feeling that casual browsing would be out of the question.

Their first stop was the Copper Mountain Chocolate

shop, where they each bought a chocolate cowboy boot. Ella's eyes all but rolled back in her head as she took her first nibble. "This is—"

"Incredible," Jenna finished for her. She let out a breathy sigh and then took another small bite.

"I'm getting more," Avery muttered before doing an abrupt about-face. "We can keep them in the fridge."

Each off them bought more chocolates, then headed back out to the sidewalk as a band started playing a catchy country song. Jenna smiled. "We danced to this."

There was no question as to who she meant by "we." Ella just hoped that T.J. was as smitten as Jenna. If he broke her heart...well, it was none of her business. She didn't want people running interference for her, so she needed to return the favor.

The three women took their time strolling the festive downtown area, browsing through the unique merchandise displayed on the sidewalks, stopping at booths to watch little kids play games.

After a few minutes at the face-painting booth, Avery said, "Come on, Jen. Get a daisy on your shoulder. It would be cute."

Jenna went red at her sister's comment, and Ella didn't think it was because she was embarrassed by the thought of a daisy on her shoulder, but rather by the thought of a certain bull rider discovering it.

"I'll do it," Ella said. A few minutes later she pulled the

shoulder of her boatneck tee down and the smiling high school girl painted a perfect flower near her shoulder, just high enough to peek out of the shirt.

"This is what you do when you're too chicken to get a tat," Ella said as she paid the girl.

After doing a complete circuit of the closed-off Main Street area, they headed back to the trailer in an effort to get their chocolates into the fridge before they melted. Avery sipped her huckleberry lemonade through a straw as she walked, while Ella and Jenna had finished theirs before they'd reached the bridge leading back to the fairgrounds.

"All clear," Avery said after shooting a look toward the area where the dedication of the new rodeo grounds and gorgeous copper bucking bronc had taken place. Only a few people were left, putting away chairs, and none of them were Shane or his brothers.

"I need a nap before the picnic," Jenna murmured as she opened the door to the small trailer.

"Good idea. I'll stretch out in the truck," Ella said. With the windows rolled down, it would be comfortable enough. Not that she'd sleep, but she'd have some time to herself. She was exhausted from watching the crowd, expecting Shane to appear at any moment, wondering what her reaction—and his—would be.

The truck would be a safe place to gather her thoughts, steel herself for what lay ahead. Because she and Shane had a few matters to discuss before she told him goodbye for real.

ELLA WAS NOT a game player. If she'd come to Marietta to see him, she'd eventually seek him out. If she hadn't, she wouldn't. All Shane had to do was to bide his time to discover which it was.

The wait was killing him. As was having Ella close by. He shouldn't have let things go as far as they did before ending them. But it had been so easy when he felt so natural around her. When they meshed so well.

Summer thing. They hadn't had to deal with any harsh realities.

He arrived at the barbecue late, having driven back to the ranch to tend to a few matters before hooking up the trailer and bringing it in so that he could spend the night. The barbecue ended at eight, but the party tended to go on.

He parked on the opposite side of the lot from the Glenn sisters' trailer and then took a second to straighten his shirt collar before locking the truck and heading to the park. Once there, he bypassed the food booths—no easy task given the amazing aromas that beckoned him to stop—and headed to the area of the park closest to the courthouse, to meet up with his brothers who were just finishing up their meals.

"I thought the agreement was that I would go back to the ranch and you guys would wait for me."

"This is just our first pass," Cody said, getting to his feet.

Zach nodded his agreement and Shane said, "Well, in that case, you're forgiven." He'd probably have to eat his second plate of food alone, but he could deal.

They'd just reached the food line when Cody gave him a nudge and he lifted his gaze to see Ella sitting on a blanket in the shade of a big elm tree with the Glenn sisters and T.J. He pulled in a sharp breath, then let it out slowly as Jenna laughed and touched T.J.'s arm and he smiled back at her.

"Did you know she was here?" Cody asked in a low voice. "Ella, I mean."

"I knew who you meant, and she *is* following the circuit," Shane muttered. Zach wouldn't have discussed the matter of his relationship with Ella with Cody, which meant that Cody had pieced things together on his own.

"So, no."

"No," Shane said on a breath. "It doesn't matter. I'm good with it."

"Keep telling yourself that."

Shane gave his brother a dark look. "If you don't drop it, I'm going to punch you in the face," he said mildly.

"She's a nice girl."

Shane pulled back his fist and Cody raised his hands. "I've seen the two of you together. I think you're crazy for sending her on her way."

"How do you know it wasn't mutual?"

"Because I also saw the way she looked at you."

That's it, big brother. Insert the knife. Give it a solid twist.

"We drop this. Now." Shane gritted the words out from between his teeth and Cody, sensing a fist was about to make contact with his teeth, did indeed drop the matter.

Now if Shane could just stop thinking about it.

He followed Cody through the line, nodded and smiled at the members of the booster club as they offered him corn on the cob, the most excellent coleslaw, and his choice of a hamburger or hotdog. He'd paid for one of each, took both, then followed his brothers to the place they'd staked out, out of sight of Ella's blanket. By the time he went for his second pass at the coleslaw and some dessert, she was gone.

Fine. Now he could eat in peace. Except that he couldn't.

He had some serious work to do on his waiting game—a fact that was hammered home when he caught sight of Ella's distinctive hat near the bridge. She was heading back to the rodeo grounds.

And so was he.

Enough waiting. He wanted to find out exactly what the deal was.

~

ELLA GLANCED OVER her shoulder after crossing the bridge to see if Avery and Jenna were behind as they were supposed to be, only to have her heart stop when she spotted Shane coming after her.

She had two choices. Stand or run. And since she'd come to Marietta to make both a stand and a point, she turned to face him full-on, setting a hand on one hip in a nonchalant way as she waited for him to catch up. He did not hurry. Each step he took toward her was steady and measured, and the way his unrelenting gaze locked on to hers, she almost felt as if they were about to have a gunfight rather than a questionable reunion.

At least her heart wasn't racing. Instead it was attempting to pound its way out of her chest like a prisoner begging to be set free.

When Shane got close enough for her to see the color of his eyes, she turned her head to give him a sideways look. But she did not say one word. He was the one running her down. He could start the conversation.

But when he stopped a few feet away from her, he didn't seem to have anything to say.

So Ella started the ball rolling. "You want to know why I'm here."

"I assume," he said slowly, "that you're here for the same reason you were at all the other rodeos."

"It is a free country," she said softly. "And I do want to collect more data."

He folded his arms over his chest, pressed his lips together briefly. "I thought we should talk instead of dodging each other."

"Who's dodging?" she asked innocently and was gratified to see the color start to rise from his collar.

"I thought about it," he said.

Score one honesty point for Shane.

"I think you purposely sent me away before." Now they were tied in the honesty columns *and* they were at the meat of the matter.

"If I did, I had a reason."

"That you never shared."

"I told you I wasn't in a place to start a relationship."

She gave him a fair's-fair look. "I'm *not* here to ask for more than you can give."

"Then…" He gave her an openly cautious look. From behind him a man called his name, but he didn't turn.

Her adrenaline-driven aura of self-possession was starting to waver, but she forged on. "I want you to tell me you *didn't* send me away to protect me from something."

He gave her a shocked look, which told her that she might just be on the right track. He may well still be mending a broken heart from Darcy Whoever. Or maybe he didn't want a repeat of the incident. His insistence that she not change her life for him ate at her.

Another shout and Shane raised his hand to let the man calling his name know he'd heard him. Ella bit her lip in frustration. She wanted an answer, but what kind of answer could she get when that guy coming toward them wasn't slowing down one bit?

"We'll talk later," Shane said in a grim voice. "Tomorrow after my ride."

"I'll put you on my schedule between interviews." She was only half kidding. T.J. had lined up an interview with a local bull rider before the rodeo, and she really hoped to catch up with one particular bull rider—Cody Starr, whom she just discovered had given a huge amount of money to a local woman to help pay for her son's heart operation. That guy needed to be questioned.

"Ella..."

She lifted her chin and smiled at the man who'd almost caught up with them, but she didn't feel like staying to make chitchat with a stranger. "I'll see you tomorrow, Shane. After your ride. Good luck."

SHANE RECOGNIZED MORE than one competitor when he walked into Grey's, intent on taking the edge off. After ordering a draft, he headed toward the table where Boone Telford, Flynn O'Connell and Cody Starr were deep in conversation. Something was up with Boone. He'd given Shane his usual sincere congratulations on the ride, but...something had been off.

Looking for a distraction from his own dark thoughts, he decided to see what the deal was with Boone. He joined the group and it took about a nanosecond to discover that Boone was having woman trouble. What would that be like?

This was not a topic he wanted to pursue, so instead he put on his game face, acted like cutting a woman loose was no big deal—even though he knew through firsthand experience that it was a total fucking big deal if a guy happened to care about the woman. Boone's reaction to his ribbing had been too serious. He cared.

Welcome to the club, bud.

Shane said his goodbyes to his fellow riders and headed to the opposite corner of the room where he spotted T.J., probably waiting for Jenna. Which meant that coming to Grey's to take the edge off had been a big mistake. But he had his beer, and he wasn't about to abandon it, so he ambled over to T.J.'s table.

"I don't often see you alone anymore." Translation—is Jenna Glenn joining you?

"Yeah. Jenna's off doing some kind of shopping with her sister. Then they're meeting me here."

Shane hooked a chair leg with his boot and pulled it out to take a seat. If Ella showed up, then, cool. It was a free country as she'd said earlier. They'd still talk tomorrow as planned and tonight they would…

The thought slowed and then sputtered out as he spotted Ella a few tables away talking to Austin Harding. The bull rider. The American Extreme bull rider.

The one who Darcy'd had a teasingly open crush on while she and Shane had been dating.

Well, shit.

He wasn't supposed to feel like jumping out of his seat and heading across the room to insert himself between the two of them—but that was exactly what he wanted to do. And what the hell…was that a little flower showing from under the edge of her shirt?

"Did you hear about Cody Starr?"

T.J.'s question jarred him abruptly back to the present. Cody Starr was a cousin by marriage, so Shane turned his attention back to the bull rider, hoping whatever it was wasn't bad news.

"No. Everything okay?"

"No telling," T.J. said before taking a drink of beer. "He fucking gave away his purse from the Reno rodeo."

"No shit." Shane gave T.J. a hard look. "You sure about this?"

"Totally. There's some lady here whose kid needed an operation. He helped her pay for it."

"Huh." Shane shot another look in Ella's direction, then focused on T.J. again, who gave him a sympathetic "sorry that your girl's with another guy" look.

"She's interviewing him," Shane said, surprising himself.

He needed to get out of there, focus on his ride. If he stayed in Grey's he'd either do something he regretted, or mess his head up so badly that he wouldn't be focusing on this ride with the proper intensity…kind of like what had happened the last couple times he'd mounted a bronc.

Shane drained his beer a little too fast, set his glass on the table and shoved his chair back. "I'm having an early night," he said. So what if he sounded like a pussy. He'd be a pussy who had a great ride tomorrow.

He'd also get out of the bar while Ella was focused on

her famous bull rider. He wasn't really running—he was simply avoiding trouble.

MOST WOMEN ELLA knew would have given their eyeteeth to spend half an hour talking to Austin Harding. And yeah, the guy was mega hot, but he was also very taken.

And he wasn't Shane.

What was going to happen tomorrow when they talked? Would he insist on cutting her loose? Because if so, then she didn't see many options—

"Ella?"

She blinked at Austin, who watched with a smile in his eyes as she came back to the present.

"I'm so sorry. I had a sudden thought."

"Must have been a doozy."

"Yeah," she said weakly, gripping her pencil a little tighter. "So looking back on your career, and the injuries sustained, would you go into it again knowing what you know now?"

The bull rider thought for a moment, then met her gaze. "You know...bull riding gave me an identity I wouldn't have otherwise had. I got money and fame, too, but you know what?"

Ella raised her eyebrows, expecting to hear the first words of regret that she'd encountered during her summer of interviewing. "What?"

He gave her a crooked smile and reached for his beer. "I'd do it again in a heartbeat. The adrenaline rush is worth it. The feeling when you've matched or beaten a one-ton adversary...can't be described. I'd do it all over again. Yes."

"All righty then." Ella slowly closed her notebook.

"And bull riding helped me hook up with my fiancée and that's probably the most important thing I got out of the deal."

"Lucky you." Ella was totally sincere and thought she'd done a good job of hiding the edge of jealousy she felt hearing that Austin had gotten his happily ever after.

Austin glanced at his phone, then gave Ella a quick smile. "It's been great talking to you. I gotta meet my lady."

"I really appreciate the interview," she said.

"If you need more, just give a shout." He got up out of his chair, touched his hat and headed for the door. Ella looked down to gather her things, then looked up again when the chair Austin had been sitting in scraped back. A smirking cowboy sat down. One she'd seen from a distance at some of the other rodeos. After watching him in action, it had seemed like a good idea to keep her distance.

"Hey," he said as he sat his glass of whiskey on the table. "I hear you're looking for rodeo competitors to interview."

Ella pulled a long breath in through her nose. "I'm focusing on bull riders, Mr.—"

"Dean. Dean Maynard." He leaned his forearms on the table bringing his face closer to Ella's. He was a guy who obviously thought well of himself, and he was good-looking enough in a chiseled, kind of smarmy way. "And I happen to know that you've interviewed a few competitors who don't ride bulls."

The way he said "interviewed" made Ella want to pop him. If he said something else in that tone, she would.

"Yes. Well. That's kind of my business."

Dean leaned back in his chair and gave her a narrow-eyed look. "You gonna interview that woman, I suppose?"

"Woman?"

His lip curled. "You know. The iron tit."

Ella laughed. She hadn't heard that term in a long time, a term used by cowboys who were intimidated by a woman who could do a man's work as good as a man. "CJ? I interviewed her before she got her pro ticket. She's awesome."

And you aren't.

Ignoring Dean's fierce frown, she gathered her purse and stood up. "I have to go." She smiled, but only because she was escaping without hurting her knuckles on the guy's smug chin. With a nod, she headed for the door.

The warm evening breeze wafted over her as she left the bar and stood for a moment looking up and down the street. There was still a lot of activity in the little town, but Ella had a full, possibly emotional day ahead of her. Best if she went to bed and rested up, because who knew what the next day might bring?

The only thing she did know was that she and Shane would have a better understanding of their situation before Saturday ended.

Chapter Fifteen

HE HAD THIS.

After his fuckups last week, other riders were getting dangerously close to his point total, and he couldn't let that happen. Two rides this week, two rides next in Great Falls and he'd sew this thing up. At the Montana finals, he'd be the guy mounting the platform with B.B. Gilmore, taking the oversize check.

But first…

Shane eased onto his bronc, worked his glove into the handle of the Barstow. Beneath him the horse shifted irritably. Testy bronc. He pounded his glove, set his feet, then gave a nod. He'd discovered early on that the longer a guy waited, the more likely he was to mess up his head.

Tiny Dancer turned out of the gate and then pounded the ground with all fours, hunching her back and dropping her head as she went aloft. She twisted, kicked, threw her head sideways, tried to turn her belly up. This horse loved to buck. And Shane held on, the rhythm of his spurs matching every move the horse made. When the buzzer sounded, he cracked his elbow open, pulled his glove free, and in one of those perfect moments that happened every now and again, rode the momentum of Tiny Dancer's last buck and sailed off the horse, landing on his feet.

It jarred the hell out of his knee and he almost went down, but somehow managed to keep upright. Grabbing his hat, he threw it into the air.

Son of a bitch!

What a ride.

The hometown crowd thought so, too, as did the judges.

Grinning widely, he stooped to scoop up his hat as he limped to the man gate. Three more rides and he'd have this thing sewed up.

He could do three.

The gateman clapped his shoulder and Shane nodded his thanks as he left the arena.

Now…the talk with Ella.

That was going to be a thousand times harder than this ride had been. He collected his rigging, watched the remaining rides, decided he had the event sewed up for today and headed for his trailer.

"Great ride, Shane."

The too-familiar voice brought his head around and he found himself face-to-face with Darcy and Cal. The happy couple. He swallowed before he could stop himself. Cal was decked out in his fancy boots, which cost more than Shane would ever dream of spending on footwear, and instead of wearing her usual shirt and jeans, Darcy wore a dress that looked as if it had stepped from the pages of an upscale western fashion magazine along with bright pink and turquoise boots.

And she looked good. Like she was born to wear dresses like that.

Ella could also wear such a dress.

"Thanks." Shane turned his attention from his ex to his business manager. "Nice boots," he said to Cal.

Cal gave Shane an odd look. "Yeah. Special-occasion boots."

"Maybe you can wear them to the wedding." He met Darcy's gaze and attempted a good-loser smile. "Congratulations," he said, hoping he sounded sincere. He was—for the most part. He and Darcy were never meant to be and now she was so much better off.

"Thank you, Shane. Will you come to the wedding?"

"Of course," he said as if it wasn't any kind of an issue at all. As if she hadn't turned his life upside down and made him realize that he needed to step up to the plate before it was too late. "Hey, I'll see you two. I have to get some ice on my shoulder."

Darcy gave him a look, telling him that she remembered those days. He worked up one final smile and limped on.

First the ice, then he'd find Ella, if she didn't find him first.

ELLA WATCHED SHANE'S ride from the grandstand with his friends and neighbors, jumping to her feet and whooping with the rest of the crowd when he'd landed on his feet after that amazing ride. She felt as if she'd been there with him through every buck and jump, and had to take a moment to catch her breath before working her way down from the stands to meet up with him.

Maybe the ride would lighten his mood.

But his mood wasn't the problem. The problem was one of communication and being straight with her. If he parted company with her because he didn't feel it, fine. Her heart would crack, but she'd move on. However, if he felt about her the way she felt about him, and was being brave…well, she wasn't going to have it.

Ella made her way around the competition area and headed for Avery's trailer. Both of her travel partners were warming up their horses for their event, so she'd have a moment to collect herself before heading to Shane's trailer, where she assumed he'd be waiting for her.

As she rounded the nose of the trailer parked closest to the tiny Easter egg she called home, she spotted a man sitting on the metal step beneath the door. A man who was not T.J. or Shane. Her steps slowed as her brain worked to come up to speed. It couldn't be…

Mitch raised his head and Ella let out an astounded breath. Oh yeah, it was her brother, sitting on the stoop, his elbows resting on his knees.

"Elle." He got to his feet and met her halfway, giving her a brotherly hug.

Ella stepped back. "Not to be rude, but what are you doing here?"

"Came to see my little sis."

Ella did a mental calculation. "Aren't you gathering right now?" Which involved days of combing the hills on their allotment, looking for cattle, which they'd bring to the ranch for the fall branding.

"Finley has a friend taking my place."

Ella lifted her eyebrows. Gathering was one of Mitch's favorite parts of ranching. He lived to beat the countryside, looking for cattle and whatever else he could find. Once he'd brought home a hundred-year-old pistol that some cowboy had been unfortunate enough to lose decades before.

"That seems unusual," she said in a dark tone.

Mitch shifted his feet.

"I'd ask you to come inside to talk, but it's hot in the trailer and you won't fit."

Her brother smiled, but his expression was way too serious for her liking.

"Why are you here?" she asked flatly.

"Ella, what the hell are you thinking turning down that internship you wanted so badly just a couple months ago?"

"It's not the same internship. I'd have to change my course of study."

"Will it pay for your education? Are you that married to

bull riders and risk?"

"It's not what I want to do right now." Ella set a fist on her hip. "Did you drive a good twelve hours to ask me about this? When you could have *called*?"

"I'm worried about you. We're *all* worried about you."

Ella's gaze widened incredulously. "What the hell? You were the one who told me just a couple weeks ago to have some fun." He'd walked to the truck with her before she'd left the ranch, and told her that he kind of understood what she was doing, and that maybe she did need to loosen up and enjoy life a little. It had been a sweet moment, and at the time Ella had been glad that at least one member of her family was starting to have some faith in her. Apparently that faith wasn't the lasting kind.

"But not to throw away a sure thing. Come on, Ella. You would have been dancing around the room had this happened a few months ago."

"I've changed."

"I know." He pointed a finger at her. "When someone changes this radically in such a short time, it's cause for concern."

She pointed back at him. "Maybe it's been percolating inside of me for a long, long time and I was just afraid to let it out. I'm not afraid anymore." She couldn't have named one particular reason for the change, but damn it, she *had* changed. "You can't say on the one hand that you want me to loosen up and then on the other, yank me back because I am loosening up."

"Maybe we're all a little afraid that you don't know how to handle your newfound super power."

Ella smirked at him. "Nice analogy, Mitch. Very colorful. But the fact of the matter is that I'm going to do what I want." A bad feeling swept over her, and her voice took on a steely edge as she said, "Do not for one minute think that you can strong-arm me into going back to the ranch." Where she would no doubt be the subject of a well-meaning familial intervention.

Mitch let out a breath, giving her the impression that she was the most exasperating person he'd encountered in a long, long time, which couldn't be true because he lived in the same house as Finley.

"Stop now," she said. "Before we get into a serious argument. Stay and enjoy the rodeo, then go home and tell the family that I'm fine."

"I would if I believed you're fine."

"I'm fine," she said from between gritted teeth. Or she was until he showed up and made her worry about the family in a way she'd never worried before. Heaven help her, she worried about them worrying about her.

And that pissed her off, as did Mitch's next question.

"Do you know where you'll be in the next month?"

"No. But, bottom line—that's my concern, not yours."

SHANE DIDN'T MAKE it back to his trailer immediately after his encounter with Cal and Darcy as planned, due to a chance meeting with a television crew who wanted to film him for the Bozeman news. He was still wearing his dusty arena clothes and carrying his gear when he approached the backside of Ella's trailer, but he figured she wouldn't mind. She'd seen him at his worst, after he'd screwed up at Red Rock, so victory dust shouldn't matter.

All he had to do was convince her that he'd been nothing but straight—hell, he might even let go with the full-on truth, while the evidence Darcy had presented of a much better life was still fresh in his brain. Then Ella could move on.

As would he.

He and Boone were facing the same fucking issues. He hoped Boone was handling matters better than him. The trouble with summer romances was that, as fun as they were, they could still leave a mark. This one had, anyway. A mark that showed no signs of fading anytime soon, but Shane knew what he had to do.

He started toward the front of the trailer, then slowed when he heard voices—Ella's voice, to be exact, and one other.

He'd probably go to hell for it, but Shane stopped just shy of the corner and listened, trying to get a feel for what he was about to walk in on. There was a taut edge to Ella's voice as she said, "If this were Finley, would you be reacting like this?"

The guy hesitated for a split second too long before saying, "Yes. I would."

"Liar," Ella muttered.

"Ella, there's crazy and then there's crazy. For you anyway."

"Do you have any idea how insulting that is?" Ella sputtered back.

Shane figured he had two choices—advance or retreat. Ella was angry, that much was clear, but he also heard the edge of pain in her voice and that was his undoing. He made noise with his boots before continuing on around the trailer, where he found Ella facing off with a tall, rangy cowboy. A guy who was striking enough in the looks department for Shane to consider being jealous for a split second. Then the family resemblance hit him. Ella's brother, Mitch Etxeberri. Here to rescue his little sister, apparently.

"Ella," he said, giving her the once-over to make sure she was okay. A guy could only fight so many protective instincts before one busted through. "You want to set a time for that, uh, interview?"

"Yes. Of course. I assume you know Mitch."

Mitch gave Shane a frowning look, as if suspecting him of some major crime.

"We never officially met," Shane said. "We competed together in college national finals in Bozeman."

"I don't remember you," Mitch said. "You'll have to excuse that. I had a head injury. Sometimes my memory of past events isn't what it should be."

"You have no reason to remember me. I only competed for one year before I dropped out of school and went pro." Fucked up his life. Like that.

"Nice to know it's not me for once."

Ella had the oddest expression, as if she wanted to protect each of them from the other. Okay…

Shane gave her a quick nod. "I need to get some ice on the shoulder, clean up. Maybe we can talk later."

"I'll find you," Ella said. "After the rodeo sometime. I'm…" she bit her lip, shot a quick look at her brother "…not sure when."

Shane's mouth flattened before he was aware of the movement. She was second-guessing herself. He knew that feeling. Hated it.

He touched the brim of his hat, then headed back around the trailer. He was familiar with the havoc well-meaning relatives could wreak, being the youngest and the most managed of the three Marvell boys, and he felt for Ella. She was an adult and could go her own way, make her own choices.

The irony of the thought slammed into him as he unlocked his trailer door.

He shoved the realization aside, told himself his situation was different, then dumped his bag inside the door and headed for the ice bag waiting for him in the tiny freezer.

Yeah. His situation was way different.

ELLA HAD HOPED to run down Cody Starr before the rodeo ended to see if she could ask him a few questions before the weekend was over. She'd had no luck finding him, so instead she and Mitch—who'd agreed to drop things for the time being—had spent the afternoon with Jenna and Avery once again checking out what the downtown area had to offer. After her second margarita mule in Rosita's restaurant beer garden, Ella's eyelids began to droop. She suspected it was more from stress than alcohol, but regardless, a nap would help.

"I'm going back to the trailer." She pointed a finger at her brother. "You are not."

"I've said what I came to say," he replied evenly, ignoring the perplexed look Avery sent his way. "Now I'm going to enjoy the rodeo."

Ella did not for one minute believe it would be that easy. Mitch might have said what he had to say, but he wasn't above repeating himself if he thought it might sway her into heading back to school, where no one had to worry about her.

She gave him a tight smile, then left the beer garden, keeping an eye out for Shane and/or Cody Starr. It was a gorgeous early fall day, and the sun made her just a little too warm as she walked the short distance to the rodeo grounds.

She resisted the urge to walk past her trailer and knock on Shane's door. After Mitch, she wasn't ready for another showdown. She'd come here to sort things out with Shane, and instead was defending herself to her brother. She'd told Shane she'd find him, and she would—when she was ready. She pressed the back of her hand against her mouth as she entered the trailer, then sank down on the nearest bunk. After she had a good sleep, she'd deal with both of them.

The thought barely entered her brain before she drifted away.

She had no idea how long she'd slept—it could have been five minutes or five hours—when a text woke her.

We got a table for the dinner.

Ella pushed her hair back from her face and sat up on the bunk. Table for the dinner? She'd slept a lot longer than she'd intended.

Be there shortly.

Unless Shane was at his trailer. In which case, she wouldn't. It was time, while her brain was fresh. First things first. Life-changing conversation, then steak.

SHANE DEBATED LONG and hard before he left the park, but once his decision was made, he didn't look back. He ducked away from the crowd and headed for the fairgrounds. Once there, he went straight to the Glenn trailer where he suspected Ella might be, since she wasn't at the festivities. He'd just raised his hand to knock when she opened the door. Her eyes went wide at the sight of him, as if she'd been thinking about him and somehow conjured him up.

"I thought we could discuss a few things while the others are at dinner."

"How do you know they're at dinner?"

"The best way. I left them there. My brothers have no idea where I am, and your brother and friends are in line for steaks."

"Thus leaving us without a chaperone. Or three."

"Yeah."

Ella pressed her lips together and glanced down at her boots. When she looked back up, he held out a hand. "Let's go to my trailer. I don't think anyone will come looking for us there."

Once they started this conversation, he didn't want to be interrupted—again. The safest place to talk was in his living quarters with the door locked.

Ella ignored his hand, but stepped down out of her trailer, locking the door behind her. "I agree."

They walked side by side the short distance to his tin can abode, and he opened the door for her. Once they were inside, he waved her to a seat, but remained standing himself, even though it stressed his knee.

"I heard your conversation with you brother."

He could tell that was not the opening she'd expected. "You did?"

"Not entirely on purpose."

She wrinkled her forehead. "Just a little bit on purpose?"

"Yeah." That summed it up well. "I understood what he was saying."

Ella's expression grew defiant, but he held up a hand, telling her to wait a moment before exploding on him.

"Because it was exactly what I'd said to you. It just...sounded different coming from someone else's lips."

He stopped, glanced down, uncertain how to continue. He wanted to be honest. He did not want to hurt her, but he didn't want the Darcy thing all over again.

"You asked if I was trying to protect you. Of course, I was. I care for you. But..." His mouth flattened. How the hell was he supposed to articulate this next thing? "I was protecting me as much as I was protecting you."

Ella's eyebrows drew together, but a few silent seconds passed before she said, "How so?"

"I wasted more than half a decade chasing buckles. I have nothing to show for it except a pickup truck and a bedroom in a house with only one bathroom."

"You think that's where you'll be for the rest of your life?"

"I think that's where I'm going to be for quite a while. I plan to train for a job I can do while still pitching in at the ranch, but I don't know what that is and if I don't win that bonus money, I'll have a hard time financing it."

"How were you protecting yourself?"

His face started to feel warm when he said, "I didn't want to go through the hell of having you decide I was a loser."

She blinked at him. "Settling for the status quo, when you could do something about it is what makes you a loser."

He was still working on that unexpected response when she rose to her feet and crossed the small space that separated them, doing exactly what he didn't want her to do, because he truly felt powerless to stop himself from responding. She took his face between her palms. "I don't want anything right now except for you to keep an open mind."

"That's it?"

"That's enough. Do not close the door. Leave it cracked open until we both decide what it is we want and need in life."

He knew what he wanted—it was standing right in front of him. He also knew what he needed—to be in a place where he felt worthy.

"I'll try," he whispered, dropping his head down to kiss her soft lips.

"Yeah," she murmured against his mouth. "You do that."

Chapter Sixteen

ELLA'S UNQUESTIONING ACCEPTANCE of who he was, and, more than that, *where* he was in his life, boggled Shane. After he'd convinced himself that he couldn't get serious about anyone until he'd gotten serious about his future, it was hard to believe that someone would be willing to work with him—the way he'd assumed Darcy would work with him.

But deep down he was glad that he had that B.B. Gilmore bonus all but sewn up, so that he was in control of his own destiny, instead of being dependent on the ranch and his brothers. If he wasn't in that position…yeah. Probably a little harder to leave that door cracked open.

He'd been set to meet Ella for the pancake breakfast, but when he arrived, he saw her talking to Cody Starr. She was fascinated by the fact that Cody had given up a huge amount of money to help with a kid's medical treatment, and even more fascinated when Shane had explained that he and Cody were cousins by marriage, via the Sweetheart, Montana, branch of the family.

"You know him?"

"The same as I know the other guys on the circuit."

"But you're cousins."

"My cousin, Brett, is his cousin." Therefore, he hadn't been able to give Ella a real starting point, so she'd researched Cody Starr on her phone while the two of them had sat in lawn chairs under the stars and listened to the bands playing in the park across the river.

It felt so damned good not to have a huge wedge between them that it kind of scared him. As did the possibility that she might suddenly come to her senses.

CJ Cooper was warming up as he made his way behind the chutes and made it a point to go over and wish her luck with her event. Saddle bronc didn't start until almost an hour after his event, but she was probably working off nervous energy—or maybe distracting herself from some of the guys nearby. That asshole Dean Maynard had been giving her shit for the entire tour and he'd turned it up a notch lately. Yesterday, it'd been all Shane could do not to deck him behind the chutes when he'd made an uncalled for "eight inch" remark.

"Thanks." She gave him a quick look, then smiled when she realized he wasn't blowing smoke. He really wanted her to do well. "You, too, Shane. Awesome ride yesterday."

"Thanks."

Tyson had tapped out the day before, so Shane was pulling his own rigging that day. It took longer to do it alone and get it just right, but he was okay with it. The methodical prep work helped him get into his head—which he was abruptly yanked out of when a feminine voice said, "You want some help today?"

He turned to see Ella standing on the platform behind him.

"How good are you?"

"You can ask my brother."

One corner of his mouth quirked up. "He did okay."

"Until the accident, yes."

The accident that had left him dealing with memory issues. But he seemed all right otherwise. He'd stopped by to say good night the previous evening, and hadn't seemed to feel the need to punch Shane out or anything for leading his little sister astray.

"I could use some help." There was something about being with Ella that made his intentions of proceeding cautiously go all to hell. "How'd your interview go with Cody Starr?"

"It was brief. He's not a man of a lot of words." She frowned a little. "I'm trying to decide if giving away that money qualifies him for the financial risk domain, impulsive risk domain, or if he's just one helluva decent guy behind all that bad-boy bravado."

"The last." He smiled down at her, wanting very much to kiss her, but bareback riders did not kiss their rigging partners. Not behind the chutes anyway.

"I'll head to the other side," she said as he lifted his rigging.

"Thanks." He lifted his chin at the chute boss to indicate that Ella was to be let through the gate.

And how crazy was it that he'd woken up yesterday morning with the solid intention of standing strong, and now Ella was helping him rig a bronc?

AFTER SHANE WAS set to ride, Ella made her way to the opposite side of the arena, where Mitch had saved her a seat in the grandstand. He gave her an odd look as she sat next to him—one she chose to ignore. Mitch was having none of it.

"Is he the reason you came to Montana?" *He* obviously being Shane. Of course, Mitch had seen her working the rigging.

"Nope," Ella replied matter-of-factly. "He's the reason I didn't leave."

It took Mitch a second to digest her quick answer. "Are you throwing away an internship for a man?"

Ella gave him a cool look. "As I see it, I'm choosing between opportunities. The one I chose doesn't pay, but I would forever regret not seeing where it takes me." Thank you, CJ, for saying the words that would help shape her life.

Ella could feel her brother studying her profile, but she chose to watch chute number six, the one Shane would buck out of. Finally she drew in a deep breath and gave him a look. "I am not going off the deep end. I am making careful choices. My objectives have changed."

Mitch cleared his throat and made a gesture in the direction of the chutes. "Should I ask about your objectives?"

"Only if you're not afraid of the answer."

"Life was easier when you were afraid of the answer," he muttered. "What is the answer?"

"Sometimes you just know stuff, Mitch. I've ignored my instincts every single time I felt this way, and took the safe path. And every time I regretted it. This time I'm going with my gut."

"So you aren't doing this because I gave you permission to go bonkers when I was in the hospital."

"Is that what you thought?"

"A little."

"So you came here to save me?"

"Maybe. I wanted to make sure you knew what the hell you were doing and why," he muttered. The lady next to him was trying not to look like she was listening, but she gave Ella a quick sideways look. Did Ella know what she was doing? Ella caught the lady's eye and nodded to her.

"I can't help wanting to save you," Mitch muttered. "The rest of us have had lots of practice screwing up. You're a newbie."

"I don't need to be saved." She hard-eyed him. "You'd do well to remember that." The woman gave Ella a satisfied nod.

Before Mitch could respond, the tractor grooming the arena left through the main gate and the announcer fired up the PA system to welcome everyone to the new rodeo grounds.

"A fine day for a rodeo, ladies and gentlemen, cowboys and cowgirls. The first thing we need to do before we have our grand entry is to turn to the neighbor next to you and give them a good old-fashioned hello-how-are-you. Because we're all one big family in rodeo and we're all one big family here in Marietta!"

There was a lot of laughing amid the low rumble of conversation as people said hello to their seatmates. Ella smiled and nodded at the elderly gentleman next to her, who doffed his cowboy hat in reply and then she turned back to her brother as a blast of music announced the start of the grand entry. Mounted riders carrying flags circled the arena while the announcer gave thanks to the sponsors and introduced the rodeo royalty. The American flag came in after the Montana flag and everyone stood as the riders lined up in the center of the arena. Ella didn't know who was singing the national anthem, but she thought it might have been the girl who sang at the rededication ceremony on Friday. Whoever it was, her voice gave Ella shivers. The good kind.

Her heart started beating faster as the arena cleared. The first event was bareback bronc riding and Shane was the second guy up.

She'd always gotten nervous when Mitch rode, and after

her brother's accident and Shane's near miss at Red Rock, she was double nervous. But he'd done an amazing job the day before—picture-perfect in every regard. There was no reason today's ride wouldn't be more of the same.

Except that she didn't feel good about it. While she was pulling the rigging, the horse seemed twitchy. Most of the equine athletes were fairly mellow in the chutes, having been through the routine time and again, but this one had chewed the metal rail and rolled an evil eye at her.

She sucked in a breath and settled back in her seat as the first rider came out of the chute. The horse wasn't much of a bucker and the cowboy had to fan it with his hat to up his points. Maybe the rail chewer would be the same way, except that would hurt Shane and his chance of winning his bonus. He needed a horse that bucked.

And that was what he got.

The horse had barely cleared the gate when it reared and twisted, lost its footing and went over sideways, slamming Shane into the gate. The horse jumped to his feet and cantered away, the pickup men going after him to loosen the bucking strap, but Shane remained still in the dirt.

A collective gasp rippled through the crowd, but Ella was on the move and barely heard it. A strong hand captured her elbow as she reached the aisle. She tried to jerk herself free, then realized it was her brother, making sure she didn't fall as she headed down the bleacher steps at a breakneck pace.

"He's up," Mitch said near her ear. "He'll be okay."

"I need to see him."

"He's okay," Mitch repeated.

Ella didn't think so, since she could see that one of the gatemen had to support him on his way to the gate. "If he's leaning on someone, then he's not okay."

"He'll be swarmed by the medics if he's hurt. You need to let them do their job."

"I will," she muttered as they reached the lower platform and started for the exit staircase. Mitch kept a firm grip on her elbow. Maybe that was a good thing—not control, but support.

A loud round of applause told Ella that Shane had made the gate, and she felt a whisper of relief, but she knew that adrenaline and grit could get a cowboy out of an arena before he collapsed again.

Mitch broke a trail through the crowd as they headed past the main gate to the chutes, holding her arm as he led the way. He might have been contradictory lately, first telling her to loosen up, then getting all bent out of shape when she did, but damn it, he was here for her now.

As she'd feared, Shane was on his way to the medic's tent they'd just passed when she and Mitch finally reached the competitors' area, supported on one side by a burly guy in a cowboy hat. His shoulder hung loosely, making Ella grimace.

"Dislocated," Mitch said from behind her as Shane approached from the chutes. "I'm surprised he's walking." There was a note of respect in his voice.

Shane looked up, his eyes glazed over in pain. He sucked

in a breath. "Not getting the bonus, Ella." He gritted his teeth and limped the last few feet to the tent.

"That's okay," Ella murmured, wanting so much to reach out and touch him, or better yet, follow him into the tent.

Wasn't happening.

"What bonus?" Mitch asked Ella.

"The B.B. Gilmore bonus," Zach said from behind them. Ella and Mitch both turned. Zach pushed his hat back as he studied the door his little brother had just disappeared through. Then he rubbed a hand over his forehead. "I'd really hoped…"

"Yeah," Ella said softly. "Me, too."

"Guess someone's got to convince him that hitting roadblocks and having to go at things in a different way isn't the end of the world." He leveled an unwavering look at Ella.

"Yes," she said, surprised that she could find her voice. "I guess they do." She glanced over her shoulder at her brother. "They might have to convince a couple people of that."

Mitch kicked the dirt in front of him. "I'm good. Your idea of loosening up is different than what I thought you thought loosening up was."

Ella wrinkled her forehead.

Mitch put a hand on her shoulder and dropped his chin so his dark eyes were level with her own. "I'm saying that you did things we didn't expect, given your past record, but you seem to have a handle on what you're doing."

"So…?"

"Whatever you do, you know that we've got your back."

Chapter Seventeen

IF ANYONE EVER wanted to know what it felt like to have one's shoulder demolished, Shane would be able to give them a decent description. Having the dislocated bone put back into place was beyond rugged, but it always was. If he'd only suffered a dislocation, then all would be well, but hitting the fence with the full weight of the horse slamming into him had also shattered bones in his forearm, torn the labrum in his shoulder and chipped the bone near his bicep.

The bones would heal, but he'd need surgery to fix the torn labrum.

So much for winning money and using it to grow a future.

His future was clear. Pain. The ranch insurance policy would cover the shoulder surgery at 50 percent, but he had to come up with the rest. Maybe he *would* have to take a loan from Zach, but his brother wasn't exactly rolling in dough. Shane had been serious when he'd told Ella they were land rich, cash poor. If cattle prices snapped back, they'd be okay, but for now…

For now, you roll with the punches.

Shane leaned his head back against the pillow and clicked the remote to change the channel of the muted television. He was going out of his mind with boredom, but being cooped up in the hospital overnight had given him a lot of time to think. Some of that thinking might not have been the clearest, due to the pain meds, but he'd noticed a trend.

Ella never left his head.

She hadn't come to see him since he'd checked into the hospital the day before. He didn't know if she would, and the possible reasons why she might not come to see him ruined him when he allowed them to sift through his brain.

He wanted her.

He was still afraid of disappointing her. Especially now. But he remembered something Zach had told him years ago when he'd been fighting to learn the basics of bronc riding and had been just this close to giving up after getting bucked off for the umpteenth time. "If you can get through the bad times," he said, "then think how good the good times will feel."

For some reason the words kept circling in his head. If he could build something despite taking a couple giant steps backward, then how good would he feel?

Probably pretty damned good.

But he wouldn't feel complete.

WAITING TO SEE Shane had been one of the hardest things

Ella had ever done, but Zach and Mitch had convinced her that Shane would be doped up after the work that had been done on his arm and shoulder and it was no time to get into a situation where he might want to hash things out in a drug-induced haze. But she had gone to his room during the night and sat in the chair next to his bed as he slept. After nodding off herself, she'd taken the nurse's advice and had returned to the rodeo grounds to spend the rest of the night in Avery's trailer.

But now she was back and things had changed.

Shane wouldn't be unconscious. Avery and Jenna were on their way back to Dillon, and Mitch had left for Nevada early that morning after she'd convinced him that she could handle things.

She'd never felt so alone.

Shane was staring in the general direction of the muted television when she hesitated just outside the door, but he seemed to sense that she was there and turned his head to meet her gaze dead-on. He looked like hell, his face pale, his hair standing on end, and she wanted him more than anything.

"I'm glad you came," he said in a low voice.

A jolt of shock went through her. "That wasn't what I thought you would say."

"What did you think I would say?" There was an edge to his voice. Uncertainty? Join the club.

She stopped a few feet from the bed, shot a quick look

around the room, which hadn't changed since she'd left around midnight, doing her best to marshal her thoughts. "I thought you'd say something along the line of, 'Go do your internship, Ella. Don't waste your time on a broken-down rodeo rider with no future.'"

Shane frowned at her and Ella found herself holding her breath as she waited for him to agree that she should leave Montana, go back to her old life. The one she'd run from.

"Do *you* see me that way? As a broken-down rodeo rider with no future?"

Ella slowly shook her head. "I do not." She saw him *as* her future, but she wasn't ready to go there yet. Not until she found out what kind of fight she had ahead of her.

He held out a hand—his good hand. The one that wasn't covered in bandages.

She blinked at the unexpected gesture. This wasn't going as planned. Where was the dustup she'd been expecting? The stubbornness? She gave him a cautious look as she slowly put her hand in his. His fingers closed over hers, his grip strong and reassuring.

"I feel like I've known you forever, Ella."

She knew the feeling. Had it herself. But she still didn't know where this was going and the cautious side of her demanded just that—caution.

"I like being with you."

It couldn't be this easy. Not after his insistence that she was better off going her own way, so she steeled herself for the "but you need to…" which was sure to follow.

But you need to do the sane thing.

But you need to consider the future.

Instead he fell silent. A long moment passed before he locked his gaze with hers and said, "I don't want to be without you."

Ella was so shocked she almost pulled her hand free. Instead she clutched his fingers tighter. Even if she had a clue as to what to say next, she didn't know if she could force the words up out of her throat.

He leveled a heart-stopping look at her. "You have to do what's right for you. Not what your family thinks is right and not what I think is right."

"I know." The most inadequate of replies.

"Good."

"I'm staying in Montana."

Shane's expression barely shifted, but she knew him well enough to read relief in his eyes. Relief and a whole lot more. He honestly wanted her to stay, which meshed nicely with her own wants and needs.

"Are you staying with Avery?" he asked.

"I am, but that's not carved in stone."

"Meaning?"

Ella hesitated for a split second, then said calmly, "I want to be in a place where you and I can see how things develop, without putting too much pressure on either of us." There. Everything was out. Her master plan flapping in the breeze to be either embraced or shot down.

"Because a bronc rider can't stand pressure," he said dryly.

"You said you weren't ready for a relationship." Now that she had regained her equilibrium, she didn't mince words. That was the issue she was dealing with. It needed to be stated.

"I changed my mind."

The world seemed to shift beneath her.

"If you wanted to stay on the ranch while we figure things out, I'm good with that. If it's too much, then I'm good with whatever you decide is best."

"You're inviting me to move onto the ranch?"

"Jason is moving back to the Marvell North. His cabin is free. You could live there if you want, for as long as you want. It has its own bathroom. No more sharing."

"How could I say no?" Her voice was barely a whisper. Talk about moving fast, but everything felt so utterly right, that she didn't even consider hitting the brakes.

His fingers tightened around hers. "I hope you won't say no, but like I said, I'm good with whatever decision you make."

She had a feeling that wasn't the total truth—that if she turned him down, it would sting. But she wasn't about to do that.

He looked down at his useless shoulder. "Besides the company, I can use all the help I can get if I'm going to come close to pulling my weight on the ranch." He smiled up at her. "You're the best guy I've ever worked with."

A laugh bubbled up out of her throat. "I'll help you." With anything and everything.

He pulled her a step closer and she edged a hip onto the bed. "If you decide, like Darcy did, that you need more of a guarantee about what the future might hold, you can walk."

Ella couldn't see herself doing that. She leaned in to kiss him, needing to feel her mouth on his. She lightly nuzzled his lips as he brought his hand up to the back of her head, holding her and then showing her just how much he wanted her to stay. When she braced her hand on the bed and lifted her head, she said, "Do you know how much time and energy you just saved me?"

He touched his forehead to hers. "How much?"

"Well, I had all these responses ready for the many arguments I figured you'd make when I told you I was thinking of relocating to Marietta." She'd come in loaded for bears and hadn't needed any of her weapons. It was mind-boggling.

He ran a gentle hand up her arm. "You could do that, you know. Move to Marietta. It's close to the ranch."

"Not. Close. Enough."

Taking care not to bump his shoulder, she slid a hand around the back of his neck, kissed him again. Because she could.

"I'm not getting the bonus money." One corner of his

mouth quirked. "Obviously. So my plans are going to take more time than expected. But I will do what I said I would."

"I guess they call that life," Ella murmured. "My plans didn't turn out as expected and I'm starting to feel pretty satisfied with the result."

"Are you now?"

"Very. Very. Happy." She leaned back. "Of course, I'd be happier if I could have my way with you, but…" she made a gesture "…sometimes one must bow to circumstances."

"As soon as I'm a little more mobile, I promise to improve your happiness quotient."

Ella laughed. "You sound like me. Science talk."

"Yeah," he said with his killer smile. "I've been practicing. Just in case."

Ella leaned down to smooth the hair from his forehead and then gave him another long kiss.

"You may not need to be mobile," she muttered against his perfect mouth.

His eyebrows lifted as he brought his hand up to touch the side of her face. "I like the way you think, Ella."

"Yeah?"

"Yeah. That and so much more. I think we're going to do good together."

"Me, too. You know why?"

He shook his head.

"Because I can't imagine not being with you, either. And

two people of the same mind are bound to be successful in their endeavors."

"Translation?" he asked in a low voice as he splayed his fingers through her hair, making a shiver go through her as his thumb caressed her temple.

Ella smiled and touched his lips with her fingers. "I love you."

Shane gave her a devastating smile as he stroked the side of her face. "And once again," he said just before kissing her, "we find ourselves of like mind."

Epilogue

HIS LAST RODEO.

It was hard to believe it would all be over before the night ended. Shane's surgery had gone well, and he'd been fanatical about his rehab during the months between the operation and the Montana State Finals. His doctor told him he probably didn't have another season in his shoulder—but he could tackle the finals since he'd qualified. And it had all come down to this. Billings, Montana, on a cold January evening. The last ride. The decider. He might go home with a purse that he could put toward the purchase of a mobile welding outfit, or he might go home empty-handed.

But he was going home with Ella and that made life right.

From the other side of the chute, Ella finished pulling the rigging, then pushed her braid back as she headed for the man gate. As she walked by Dean Maynard, he had a feeling she wanted to shoulder-check him, but she didn't. He'd tried to make a smart-ass comment about women *pulling* rigging, the double entendre perfectly clear, as was the fact that he was a complete asshole.

Ella didn't lower herself to his level.

Instead she joined Shane where he leaned on the rails above his bronc, Thomasina. Ella didn't say a word, but allowed her shoulder to lean in to his. He'd have to mount in a matter of minutes, but this quiet time with his lady was important to him—if one could call the chaos behind the chutes quiet. They were quiet in their heads, happy in their commitment to one another.

"I should let you get to it," she said.

He nodded.

"Try to stay in the middle."

That won her a smile and he barely resisted the impulse to kiss his rigging partner. Once she was gone, he turned his attention to Thomasina. Helluva name for a horse.

"What do you say?" he murmured. The time was approaching. The national anthem had been sung and all the falderal was coming to an end out in the arena. "You go for bronc of the year and I'll win me a big purse."

The horse snorted, and Shane took it as a good sign.

He was riding second to last, and three guys had already competed their rides before Shane touched his horse, let her know he was coming, then climbed the rails. The guys helping out spotted him as he got on board, slid forward, and worked his glove into position.

The chute two away from him opened and the horse blasted out, giving Boone Telford one hell of a ride. Shane blocked it out just as he'd blocked the others. Took a couple deep breaths, shifted his body on the horse's warm back.

"Ready when you are," someone said next to his shoulder.

He gave an immediate nod and the gate flew open. He'd ridden only a couple practice rides since the surgery, not wanting to bang his shoulder up, and he was concerned about lack of practice and the integrity of his joint.

The horse surged beneath him, all muscle and sinew, stomping the ground, then twisting upward as he found his sweet spot and muscle memory took over as he balanced on the bronc, knees working better than they had in months. Due to years of experience, he knew exactly when the buzzer would sound, and a split second later he took a double grip, opened his elbow, released his glove.

Thomasina stopped bucking and cantered around the periphery of the arena, giving Shane one last victory lap. He raised his hand to the crowd, then grabbed for the pickup man. When he hit the dirt, he was all smiles—until the gravity of what was about to happen next hit him hard.

Was he up to it?

~

ELLA MADE HER way back behind the chutes as soon as Shane came out of the man gate. He looked around, spotted her, headed toward her.

Only he wasn't smiling the way he should have been after that hellacious ride. What the heck? He could win this thing.

He took her hand, led her away from the chutes toward a quiet corner, which alarmed her even more.

"Are you okay?" she asked after he released her fingers.

"Fine." He swallowed.

This was not the man she'd left behind the chutes. "You're not fine."

"I will be. I hope."

What? Ella frowned at him as he unbuttoned his shirt pocket, dug in, pulled something out, and then dropped down into a kneeling position.

Damn. Had he blown a knee?

And then it struck her.

No. Way.

She pulled in a shaky breath as he held out the ring between his thumb and forefinger and said, "Ella, this is my last rodeo. I'm leaving one life behind and embarking on another." He swallowed again. "I would like it if you came along with me."

Ella pressed her lips together to keep from crying. She wasn't a crier, and this wasn't the time to start.

"Will you do me the honor of being my wife?"

Ella lost track of what happened next. Somehow the ring ended up on her finger—a perfect fit—and she ended up in Shane's arms. After he swung her around and then set her back on her feet, she said, "You rode with my ring?" 'My ring' had a lovely sound to it.

"I did."

"I love that you did that," she murmured as she looked

down at her hand where the sapphire sparkled, then back up at him. "I love you. And for the record, yes, I'll marry you. I can't imagine another man I'd rather ride through life with."

Shane tipped her head so that he could kiss her, leaving her with no doubt about how much she meant to him.

"The ring is beautiful," she murmured against his lips.

"It's a Montana sapphire. My mom's ring. She told me she'd kill me if I lost it in the arena, so I buttoned it in."

"Good precaution," Ella said on a laugh. She'd met Shane's mom at Thanksgiving and loved the down-to-earth woman who'd raised the man she loved.

"Hey Shane!"

They both turned as the guy appeared from around the concrete column that partially blocked them from view. "You won! You got top score."

Ella whooped and wrapped her arms around Shane's neck, but all he did was smile and thank the guy who'd shared the awesome news. The man looked confused at Shane's lack of reaction, then shrugged and headed back to the action.

Once he was gone, Shane looked down at Ella and said, "I won twice tonight, and the most important win didn't involve bucking."

Ella smiled up at the man she loved. She'd won, too.

The last rodeo had been a good one.

The End

The 79th Copper Mountain Rodeo

Book 1: *The Cowboy Meets His Match* by Sarah Mayberry

Book 2: *The Bull Rider's Return* by Joan Kilby

Bok 3: *Cowboy Come Home* by Sinclair Jayne

Book 4: *The Cowboy's Last Rodeo* by Jeannie Watt

Book 5*: The Rodeo Cowboy's Baby* by Heidi Rice

Available now at your favorite online retailer!

More by Jeannie Watt

The Marvells of Montana series

The Marvell family, which has a long history in Montana and two family ranches—the Marvell North, near Sweetheart, Montana, and the Marvell Cattle Company, near Marietta, Montana.

The Marvel North Ranch

Book 1: *The Montana Bride*

Book 2: *The Christmas Secret*

Book 3: *Catch Me, Cowboy*

Book 4: *The Cowboy Rides Away*

Available now at your favorite online retailer!

About the Author

Jeannie Watt is the author of over 20 contemporary romances and the recipient of the Holt Medallion Award of Merit. She lives in a small ranching community—a place where kids really do grow up to be cowboys—with her husband, dog, cat, horses and ponies. When she's not writing, Jeannie enjoys sewing retro fashions, running, and buying lots and lots of hay.

Thank you for reading

The Cowboy's Last Rodeo

If you enjoyed this book, you can find more from all our great authors at TulePublishing.com, or from your favorite online retailer.

TULE
PUBLISHING

Printed in Great Britain
by Amazon

55434963R00154